Shine a Light

Shine a Light

An Orchard Hill Romance

Rebecca Crowley

TULE
PUBLISHING

Chapter One

ELLIE BLOOM'S SHOE broke halfway up the stairs to her apartment. One minute she was racing to her front door, the next her stiletto heel snapped clean off and her foot hit the stair hard. Her ankle twisted on impact and she sucked in a breath, her eyes watering from the flash of pain.

Then she hoisted her purse higher on her shoulder and kept going, taking the stairs two at a time.

She slammed through the door to her one-bedroom apartment, slung her purse on the table, and kicked off her shoes—or, shoe and a half.

Her fridge held the carefully curated ingredients for what the TV cooking-show host described as a decadent recipe for champagne risotto with wild mushrooms, followed by a rich, flourless chocolate cake. She had candles at the ready, a bottle of wine in the fridge, and two brand-new, pristine white plates to replace her mismatched thrift-store staples. Everything she needed for the perfect romantic dinner and, inevitably, the moment Jeff asked her to be his girlfriend.

Everything she needed—except time.

When she'd parked her budding acting career to take a

job as an executive assistant to a senior executive at a bank, she knew her work-life balance would tilt dangerously toward the former, but she was desperate. Her mom's medical bills were mounting, her brother-in-law had just been laid off, and the payout from her dad's life insurance policy was a distant memory. Her salary plugged the financial hole and kept the whole family afloat.

Then it paid for the funeral.

Now the zeroes in her paycheck piled up in a special savings account, nicknamed "Hello Hollywood" on her banking app. It had been two years since her mom died, but with each passing week she felt more ready to finally wave goodbye to St. Louis and start over in Los Angeles. She'd redone her headshots, found an agent, even taken a couple of acting classes to refresh her skills. A couple more months of saving and she would have enough to sustain her while she looked for work. As soon as that day came, she'd pull the trigger—quit her job, book the flight.

And broach the subject of continuing their relationship long-distance, Ellie supposed, belatedly remembering her almost-boyfriend.

No need to get ahead of herself—first she had to get through this evening. Her boss had an annoying habit of meandering over to her desk on his way out of the office and unloading a massive, last-minute to-do list on her, and tonight was no exception. She'd spent an hour and a half scrambling through as much as she could get done, and she'd have to go in early tomorrow to finish, but she was home with just enough time to throw something together before Jeff arrived.

Meticulously simmered risotto and tenderly baked cake were out. She yanked open the fridge and stared hard at its contents, eventually choosing the fanciest-looking meal kit from her subscription service. She could bulk it out with rice and a salad.

Hardly the Michelin star–worthy effort she planned, but desperate times.

She ripped off the cardboard cover and chucked the aluminum tray in the oven, then poured rice and water into a pot and stuck it on the burner. She had opened the cupboard in search of something dessert-ish when her phone rang.

Jeff's number flashed on the screen. She took a breath, stepped away from the range to minimize the background noise, and answered.

"Hey, you. How was your day?"

A pause. "Fine. Do you have a second?"

"Of course, I'm just putting the finishing touches on dinner. If you're caught up at the office, don't worry, I'm honestly running a little—"

"I don't think this is going to work, Ellie."

She blinked. "Tonight? That's okay, we can reschedule."

"I mean us. We're not going to work."

Ellie's heart seemed to drop into her stomach, then rise up again, borne on a swelling tide of anger and irritation.

"You're breaking up with me?"

"We weren't exactly together, but—"

"You're telling me this now? You're supposed to be here for dinner in less than half an hour. I've got a whole meal planned."

"I'm sorry, Ellie. I was thinking about this the whole day. I don't want to lead you on if I don't see a future for us, and I don't."

She closed her eyes and pinched the bridge of her nose. She hadn't necessarily imagined Jeff would be the love of her life, but she thought he'd at least be someone she could bring to the office holiday party.

Now she'd rushed home from work, run up four flights of stairs, nearly broken her ankle, wasted a bunch of money on stupid candles, and he didn't even have the decency to show up and speak to her face-to-face.

What else could possibly go wrong?

"Listen, Jeff, I don't think you…" She trailed off, sniffing suspiciously.

Was that smoke?

She whirled toward the range and gasped. She'd accidentally flung the cardboard packaging too close to the gas flame, and the corner was beginning to burn.

"I have to go." She cut the call and darted forward, her fingers just an inch from the cardboard when it suddenly caught fire. The orange flame surged upward, catching the decorative, hand-painted tea towel she'd hung there—which also promptly ignited.

"Oh no," she muttered. "Oh no."

The smoke alarm shrieked to life, and she clapped her hands over her ears as the fire spread into a raging, insatiable beast rapidly consuming her kitchen. She heard pounding on the door and found the presence of mind to grab her purse and sprint out of her apartment, nearly colliding with her neighbor, Deshaun.

He looked past her to the wall of orange flames growing bigger by the minute. His eyes widened and he kicked the door shut, then took her by the arm and rushed toward the entrance to the stairwell.

"I'll call 9-1-1," Deshaun told her, phone already in hand. "Are you all right?"

Ellie looked down at her bare feet, then blew a lock of wavy hair out of her eyes before looking up at her neighbor. "Honestly? I've been better."

ELLIE AND DESHAUN were already at the curb when the rest of the occupants of the building began spilling out onto the street, but when the first person reached them—a pissed-off-looking man in a bathrobe—and asked what happened, she simply shrugged. Her night was going badly enough—she didn't need to incur the ire of the forty or so irritated residents shivering in the December chill. Deshaun, ever loyal, also kept shtum.

A moment later a fire truck zoomed toward the building, lights flashing and horn blaring, before jerking to a halt at the curb. Ellie watched in mute horror as a team of helmet-clad men poured out of the truck and thundered into the building, her neighbors parting to clear their way.

Suddenly the enormity of the situation—the likely scale of the damage, the cost of putting it right, and the subsequent cancellation of any and all plans she had to make a clean break and start over—hit her like a sandbag. Would her insurance cover an entire building's worth of torched possessions? How would any of her neighbors ever forgive her? Ellie couldn't bring herself to turn around and look at her apartment building, terrified to see the reality of flames leaping around the jagged edges of broken windows. Instead she sat down hard, barely cognizant of the rough, cold asphalt beneath her bare feet, and put her head in her hands.

For so long she'd just about managed to hold everything together. Now it was all falling apart.

"Ma'am?" A man's voice, a hand on her forearm.

Ellie lifted her chin, unsure how long she'd been wallowing in her own personal darkness, and squinted at the firefighter crouched in front of her. Then she took all leave of her senses.

"Eliana Bloom?" he asked.

Ellie barely heard him, too distracted by the most perfect face she'd seen in a long time—maybe forever. Thick, dark hair, delightfully mussed by the helmet he'd propped under one arm. Equally dark eyes, nicely wide-set, and a soft-looking, playful mouth with a luscious lower lip she could just imagine—

"Eliana Bloom, is that you? Apartment 4C?" he asked again, snapping Ellie back to attention.

"That's me."

"The fire's out. I'll take you upstairs and walk you through the damage. It's not great, but it's not the worst I've seen."

She blinked up at him, struggling to process what he said. "Not the worst? What about all my neighbors?"

He tilted his head to the side, a single line of confusion appearing between his eyes, and she realized everyone else was slowly plodding inside, shepherded by two other fire-fighters.

"Wait, it was just my apartment? The fire didn't spread?"

He shook his head. "This is a fairly new building, so the insulation is all fire-resistant. Everyone had to evacuate for safety, but yours is the only apartment with any damage. Sorry," he added.

"No, that's great news. I thought everyone else's apartments went up in flames, too. You said I can go in and check?"

He pushed to his feet, then extended his hand to help her up off the curb. His grip was firm, warm, and steady. Their gazes met along the length of their arms, and as her bare feet flattened on the asphalt all the chill fled from her bones.

He smiled, easy and reassuring, and although the fire was out, she could've sworn she felt the heat of its flames.

She joined the crush of people squeezing through the front door and up the narrow staircase, Deshaun in front of her, Sexy Firefighter at her back. The crowd thinned as her neighbors stepped out of the stairwell to return to their apartments, and by the time she reached the fourth floor only a handful remained.

Immediately Ellie saw that her door was propped open. Deshaun touched her shoulder as they approached, and murmured, "I'm right across the hall if you need anything," before disappearing into his own apartment.

Slowly Ellie approached the entrance to her apartment, visions of apocalyptic destruction dancing in her mind. She took a deep breath, touched the mezuzah on the post for luck, and then peered around the doorframe.

It was bad.

Not quite as bad as the scorched wasteland she'd imagined, but still very, very bad.

The kitchen was a blackened mess. Charred cabinets, bits of the stove melted and warped, counters and backsplash caked in soot. The whole open-plan living room stank of thick, pungent smoke.

But that wasn't the worst of it. Evidently her apartment was fitted with a sprinkler system. On the plus side, it seemed to have limited the impact of the fire in the kitchen. The downside, however, was that it had absolutely soaked everything else she owned.

Her beloved turquoise area rug squelched under her feet. On the arm of the couch, water dripped from the ends of the blanket her grandmother had knitted. The brand-new leather tote she'd splurged on as her signing-an-agent gift to herself was full to the brim, its supple suede interior probably beyond repair.

And the soft-focus, thirty-five-year-old, smiling photograph of her mom and dad when they were dating—before the heavy expectations of marriage and children and careers, before the ugly intrusions of illness and death—was wavy and blurred and ruined on the bookshelf.

She picked up the photo gingerly, her eyes welling, cursing herself for not taking the time to get it framed, to have afforded it even that slight protection. She was just always so busy with work...

No, she told herself sternly. Enough lying to herself. She hadn't gotten it framed because some days she could barely look at it. The broad smile of the father she increasingly couldn't remember, his arm around her mom, his posture relaxed and loose, like he didn't have a care in the world.

And her mom. So young, baby-faced, yet her smile was subtle and mature, as if she knew the future wouldn't be perfect, that bumps and bruises and outright catastrophes lay ahead, but that it would all be worth it. Every awful, beautiful, unforgettable minute.

She slapped the photo back onto the shelf and pressed her hand over her mouth, stifling a sob. She missed them both so much.

"I'll leave a copy of the fire incident report for your insurance company."

The soft words were clearly not meant to be intrusive, but Ellie pivoted sharply anyway, yanked out of her reverie. She'd forgotten all about Sexy Firefighter, who stood beside her small kitchen table, which was already buckling from the water pooled in its center.

"That would be great, thanks."

"The structure is sound, but I don't think this place will be inhabitable for a while. With the water damage, the city might ask you to get a damp report before you can move back in. The building owners have been notified, and the super should be up here in a minute. They'll probably get a service company out here to drain the water and start the drying process."

She nodded as if she had any idea what the drying process could possibly entail. "Of course."

He shifted his weight. Was he hesitating? He seemed like there was a lot more he wanted to say, but he only asked, "Do you have somewhere else you can stay tonight?"

She did—and her heart sank at the thought. "My sister's. She lives in Orchard Hill. It's a suburb just past—"

"I know it well. I just bought a house out there."

Of course he had. Good-looking guy like that, probably had a fiancée and a brand-new sofa and a quirky but adorable passion for home-brewing beer in the basement. She bet Sexy Firefighter knew exactly who he was and where he was going, and never, ever gave in to even a second of self-doubt.

Must be nice.

"What a coincidence," she mused.

He smiled politely. "Well, I'll leave you to it. Any questions, feel free to call the department's main number."

"I really appreciate you and the team coming out so quickly. Please pass on my thanks."

"Sure thing." He ducked his head in a farewell gesture as he headed out of her apartment, but stopped in the doorway. He touched her mezuzah, then turned back, their gazes locking across the room.

"Did you know that some farmers burn their fields every year to prepare for planting? The fire kills all the weeds, clearing out the soil so it's ready for new seeds."

She shook her head faintly, wondering why that random fact didn't sound as weird as it should. "I did not know that."

He scanned the apartment behind her, then his gaze returned to hers. "This probably feels like a total disaster. But sometimes you have to burn it all down before anything new can grow."

She smiled weakly. "I hope you're right."

"I usually am." He winked, then rapped the doorframe

beneath the mezuzah three times before disappearing down the hall.

Ellie stood still in her apartment, silent now except for the *drip, drip, drip* of water from what seemed like every possible surface. She had nothing—no clean clothes, no salvageable food, oh, and no almost-boyfriend, although that particular mess now paled in comparison.

She couldn't remember the last time she'd asked for help from anyone, let alone her younger sister. But now she had no other choice. She had to swallow her pride and pray that firefighter was right—that this fire would finally be what pushed her out of her hometown, not drop her all the way back to where she started.

Chapter Two

ELLIE PARKED ALONG the curb in front of her sister's house and climbed out, tugging the still-damp, sooty tote she'd managed to fill with a few essentials. She shut the driver's-side door, then paused at the end of the walkway, gazing up at her sister's house.

Naomi was eighteen months younger than Ellie, but when it came to ticking off life goals, she was light-years ahead. She'd gotten engaged to her college boyfriend, Dan, the summer before she started graduate school, and they were married a few weeks after she completed her social work licensing exam. Their two sons, Gideon and Isaac, followed in quick succession and were both in elementary school. As a family they'd had a bump in the road a couple years ago when the accountancy firm where Dan worked closed its St. Louis office. Ellie thought it was a perfect excuse to move somewhere new, but instead Dan found a new job locally.

Now they lived in the same neighborhood where she and Naomi grew up, in a handsome, brick-fronted house built in 1925, which they'd worked hard to renovate and modernize. In fact they seemed to have done more since she was last here—new windows, repairs to the front steps, and totally overhauled landscaping. Seemed like a lot to get through in… When was her last visit?

Her cheeks heated with guilt. So long ago, she couldn't even remember.

Windows punctuated the brick facade, curtained rectangles of muted light, except for one. On what she knew was the dining-room sill, Naomi's family had lit the menorah, signifying the first night of Hanukkah.

Ellie bit her lower lip, her eyes focused on those two gently shimmering candles.

Her mom had loved Hanukkah, probably more than anyone. Though it was only a minor holiday in terms of its religious significance, her mom adored the story and its symbolism—the triumph of the underequipped Maccabees in their defense of the Jewish faith against the army of King Antiochus, the restoration of the temple after the fighting, and of course the miracle of the oil that kept the menorah burning for eight days. She saw the holiday as a celebration of God's constant presence, and a reminder that no matter the odds, faith would always prevail.

Until a few years ago, Hanukkah was a major event on the Bloom family calendar. They lit the menorah, exchanged a few gifts, sang and relaxed and cooked together—Ellie could practically smell the fragrant, savory latkes just thinking about it. But when her mom died, it seemed like the magic died with her. Naomi hadn't even asked if Ellie wanted to come down for Hanukkah—and worse, Ellie hadn't bothered to take her menorah out of the closet this year.

She shouldered her tote and took a deep breath. On the drive out of the city and into the suburbs where she'd spent her childhood she kept feeling like one of the little plastic figurines in a board game who'd drawn the wrong card and gotten knocked all the way back to the beginning, but this didn't have to be like that. Hanukkah wasn't really that important, not theologically—her mom's enthusiasm was disproportionate. Her apartment would be fixed and she would move back in. Whatever wasn't covered by insurance would be a hit to her savings, but that meant delaying her departure a couple of months, not years. Plus she had an agent now, and it would only take one audition to change—

The door swung open, halting her train of thought as her nephews spilled out and ran toward her, whooping with excitement. Naomi appeared in the doorway, Dan just behind her, jointly silhouetted in the warm glow from the lights inside. Ellie's tote slid to the ground as she reached down to embrace her nephews, their simultaneous chatter no less endearing for being totally incomprehensible.

"Hello to you, too," she said with a laugh, before retrieving her bag and starting up the walkway.

Naomi stood with her arms crossed, a fond smile curling her lips. "I always said you were the fiery one."

"Ha ha," Ellie replied dryly, but pulled her sister in for a hug, and then did the same for her brother-in-law.

"How bad is the damage?" Dan asked, taking her bag so she could remove her coat.

"Bad. Five articles of clothing to my name bad. In the end the fire wasn't so much the problem, it was the water from the sprinkler system."

Naomi winced, ushering her inside as the boys tore down the hallway. "Well, at least you're safe and sound. Everything else is just stuff, and we've got more than enough stuff to share."

Ellie's heart twisted as she thought of the ruined photograph, but forced a smile. "Does that include dinner? I'm starving—mine came out a little overdone."

Her sister rolled her eyes at her cheesy joke, then nodded to the kitchen. "We saved you a plate. Come tell us everything."

Twenty minutes later Ellie had a full stomach and an easier smile as she basked in the warmth, light, and energy of Naomi's family. Seven-year-old Gideon and five-year-old Isaac had hung on every word of her only slightly exaggerated tale of residential inferno, then she'd demolished a generous serving of homemade lasagna while they caught her up on the latest news from Orchard Hill—school projects, work dramas, plus the usual gossip about marriages, deaths, and births.

"Oh, and we have a new Hebrew school teacher," Isaac informed her. "Mr. Jonah. Rabbi Spellman is his dad. He's so funny."

"And he lives next door," Gideon added.

Ellie raised her brows at her sister. "What happened to Mrs. Weintraub?" she asked, referring to their former next-door neighbor.

"She moved to a seniors' community in Florida. We were a little surprised that a single guy bought the place, but it was a real wreck inside, so I guess it needed someone willing to do the work. Evidently Mrs. Weintraub kept everything exactly the same as when she moved in fifty years ago."

"The rabbi's bachelor son moves in next door and you don't even try to set me up? You're losing your touch," Ellie chided her sister.

"I didn't think he'd compete with Jeff," Naomi replied evenly.

Ellie cringed at the mention of her not-almost-boyfriend. "At this point a houseplant would win that contest."

"Probably better to be single when you hit Hollywood, anyway," Dan said encouragingly. "You'll want to meet new people and start over, not be tied down to someone back home."

"You're absolutely right. Thank you, Dan."

"When are you going to Hollywood?" Isaac asked.

"I'm not sure yet, kiddo. Hopefully soon."

"Aunt Ellie's going to be a famous actress," Naomi told the boys.

Suddenly Gideon's eyes widened. "Aunt Ellie, you know

all about acting—you should direct our Hanukkah show."

"Yeah!" Isaac agreed, as Ellie felt the color drain from her face.

"I don't know, boys. Aunt Ellie is so busy with work," Naomi offered.

"And I'm sure you already have a great helper organizing the performance," Ellie added.

Gideon shook his head vigorously. "Arielle Garber's mom was supposed to do it but she hurt her back and now she can't. Rabbi Spellman said this afternoon that if no one else volunteers, we'll have to skip it this year."

Ellie and Naomi exchanged a weighted look. Directing the Hanukkah performance—a cute, end-of-semester play on the eighth night of the holiday—had been their mom's pride and joy. Every year she came up with a new approach to the story, made most of the costumes by hand, and was usually crying happy tears by the time the last little Maccabee had haltingly read their line.

Performing in the play had been Ellie's first taste of acting, and as she got older she'd been more and more involved, helping her mom write the script, blocking scenes, and even directing portions of the show. To this day she remembered the thrill of standing in front of a roomful of parents, all eyes on her as she delivered her lines. She loved nothing like she loved theater, and the Hanukkah play was where it all started.

But directing the play now—that was a whole other story. Although she'd helped, it was definitely her mom's domain. She wouldn't know where to begin. And what if she screwed it up? What if everyone pity applauded at the end, feeling sorry for the poor woman—an aspiring actress who'd once had so much promise, even briefly been the talk of Orchard Hill when she appeared in a feature film at only eleven years old—who'd tried and failed to fill her dead mother's shoes?

No way.

"Actresses do what the director tells them, they don't come up with all the ideas for the performance. I just don't think I'm the right person, but maybe if someone else volunteers, I can help with—"

"Please, Aunt Ellie, please!" Gideon begged, steepling his hands in front of his chest. Isaac copied his older brother and, never one to be outdone, took it a step further by actually getting on his knees at her feet. Gideon joined him and upped the ante with the most adorable puppy-dog pleading face she'd ever seen, his lower lip rolled out so far she hoped he'd be able to get it back in.

Ellie glanced at her sister, who shrugged as if to say, *it's your call*, then back at the two already clearly gifted actors on the floor.

Maybe she would screw it up. Maybe she would disappoint everyone. But nothing would've disappointed her mom more than the Hanukkah play being canceled altogether, and for that reason alone, she would give it her best shot.

You're welcome, Mom, she said silently, before giving her nephews a big grin.

"You win. I'll do it."

IT WAS LATE when Ellie finally climbed the stairs to the guest room. She'd helped bathe her nephews, then read them each a story before handing them over to Dan to be tucked in. Afterward Dan opened a bottle of wine and the three of them sat around the kitchen table catching up. They'd laughed long and hard, and the night wore on quickly. Now it was nearly midnight.

She'd regret it in the morning when she had to get up extra early to commute all the way into the city, but as she shut the guest-room door and saw that her sister had left folded stacks of extra clothes and toiletries in her room, it all felt worth it.

She got ready for bed, then opened the closet to put away the clothes she'd be borrowing for the next few weeks, as well as the handful she'd salvaged from her apartment. As she reached to grab an extra hanger from the shelf, she spotted a cardboard box—and froze when she read the handwritten lettering on the outside.

Mom's Hanukkah Stuff.

Ellie hesitated, unsure whether she was ready to open a nearly literal Pandora's box of emotions and grief. Maybe tomorrow, once she'd had a good night's sleep. Or the next day—or maybe the last night of Hanukkah. Maybe she should just focus on getting through the holiday first.

Yet she found herself tugging the box down from the shelf, her hands placing it on the nightstand as if powered by some force outside her control.

She opened the box and gently parsed through the contents, swallowing hard against the sudden lump in her throat. Her mom's brass menorah, alongside which she and Naomi had lit their own as soon as they were old enough. A half-empty box of candles. A wooden dreidel, so old the Hebrew lettering had mostly worn off on each side.

And at the bottom, a stack of programs accumulated over two decades of Hanukkah performances.

Tears welled in Ellie's eyes as she opened the most recent one. Her mom had been so ill then, but they'd still had hope—it was a week later that they got the news her cancer was terminal.

Ellie remembered her mom's face like it was yesterday, so thin, her cheeks sunken and her skin sallow, but her eyes were bright and her smile brimmed with joy as she watched the children tell an old, old tale of faith and hope and miracles. At the end the rabbi had thanked their mom for her work, and the congregation had given her a standing ovation as two of the children presented her with a big bouquet of flowers.

It was one of the happiest nights they'd had as a family

since her diagnosis.

And one of the last they'd spend together outside the hospital.

Ellie sniffed hard, swiping tears from her cheeks. This would be her last Hanukkah in St. Louis, and she would make it the best if it killed her. She would put on a Hanukkah performance like the congregants of Temple Sinai had never seen. She would show them all that she was her mother's daughter. She would make her mom proud.

Ellie hefted the menorah from the box and carried it over to the windowsill. She took two candles from the tattered box and placed one in the higher, center position, and one on the farthest-right end. She dug around in the nightstand for a box of matches, switched off the lights, lit the shamash candle at the center, and began to whisper.

"Baruch atah, Adonai Eloheinu, Melech haolam, asher kid'shanu—"

Ellie stopped halfway through the prayer, the hand holding the shamash hovering above the menorah as she stared out the window.

There seemed to be a reflection in the window in the house next door—another menorah, another shamash paused midair—only it was reversed.

And as she squinted into the darkness, she realized the hand holding the shamash belonged to a man. A man who looked extraordinarily like…

"Sexy Firefighter!" she exclaimed aloud.

He smiled softly, lifting his other hand in greeting. She did the same, and instead of being awkward their raised palms felt oddly connecting, like the distance between their houses had just shrunk ever so slightly.

She started over, her voice a little stronger this time as she used the shamash to light the lone candle. "Baruch atah, Adonai Eloheinu, Melech haolam, asher kid'shanu b'mitzvotav v'tsivanu l'hadlik…"

She paused, glancing back up at her newfound companion in this ancient tradition. They shared one more smile before finishing in what she was pretty sure was unison, "Ner shel Hanukkah."

Chapter Three

S HIFTING THE BAG of a dozen bagels to one hand, Jonah raised his foot off the ground and balanced the drinks container on his knee while he used his other hand to shove his key into the lock on his parents' front door. He released the latch, turned the handle, and managed to snatch up the cardboard carrier seconds before the three steaming cups of coffee inside would've tumbled to the ground.

"Breakfast," he called triumphantly, holding the bagels and coffees aloft.

Silence.

He kicked the door shut and proceeded through the entryway to the kitchen, only stopping a couple of times to remind himself of the layout of his parents' new house. It was coming up on a year since his father had been installed as the new rabbi at Temple Sinai, and they'd rented for the first nine months before deciding on this spacious, elegant older home within walking distance of shul. Every time he visited, Jonah chuckled to himself at how fitting this place was—the meticulously maintained wainscoting and abundance of mahogany were every inch as traditional and formal as Rabbi Spellman himself.

There was no sign of his parents in the kitchen, so he put the bagels and coffees on the table and stepped through the French doors to the backyard. As he suspected his mom was on her knees in her herb garden, wireless earbuds in her ears.

"Mom," he said, and got no response. "Mom," he tried again, a little louder, before putting a hand on her shoulder.

She jerked around, then put one hand on her chest and plucked out her earbuds with the other.

"You shouldn't sneak up on people like that. Nearly gave me a heart attack." She swatted his leg playfully before she took his proffered hands and let him help her to her feet.

"I've been listening to this podcast, the Frum Fillies. They're hysterical! This week is all about how to cheat at making potato latkes and then passing them off as your own."

Jonah smiled as he walked with his mom back to the kitchen. Short, stocky, and as pragmatic as the day was long, Elaine Spellman had always been the down-to-earth anchor keeping his loftily minded father from floating straight up into space. While her husband, Avner, dedicated his waking hours to rabbinical study and temple business, Elaine kept their two children fed, watered, and shuttled around the Boston suburb where they'd lived until the job at Temple Sinai came up.

Jonah was surprised when they announced the move— Avner was well established as the assistant rabbi at a synagogue easily three times the size of Temple Sinai—but as the weeks wore on he put the pieces together. His dad was approaching sixty, and this could be his last opportunity to lead his own congregation. Temple Sinai was a welcoming, family-oriented Reform temple where he could make his mark as a theologian as well as the head of the community. The stakes were high for his dad's career—which is why he hadn't exactly wept with joy when Jonah announced he'd be moving to St. Louis in tandem.

"Your father's in his study. I'll get him—you start laying out the breakfast," Elaine instructed.

Jonah had to open three cupboards before he found the plates. He arranged them around the kitchen table as his mom's footsteps echoed down the wooden-floored hallway, then pulled two types of cream cheese from the fridge. He transferred the to-go cups of coffee into his parents' favorite mugs, set out the cutlery, then took a seat and tried to shake off the flickering nervousness that usually preceded an interaction with his father.

It hadn't always been this way. Jonah and his dad had spent his early life in mutual adoration—the wise, all-knowing father and the bright, obedient son. Everyone marveled at Jonah's academic prowess, his easy grasp of Hebrew, his capacity for theological analysis beyond his years. Avner basked in the glory of his son's aptitude, and Jonah lived for his father's praise, even when it came at the cost of playing baseball, or going to a middle-school dance, or doing anything that would prevent him from spending most of every weekend at shul.

Jonah didn't mind. He loved his faith, he loved his father, and he was going to follow in every one of his dad's— and his grandfather's, and his great-great-uncle's—footsteps until he, too, had earned the title of Rabbi Spellman.

He went to college in Chicago, graduating with a degree in philosophy. During his senior year he applied to rabbinical college in New York City, specifically choosing a program that would allow him to spend time in Israel. He knew a lot of his peers would've taken a gap year after high school to live in Israel, but he'd funded his undergraduate degree through a complex matrix of merit scholarships, loans, and financial aid, chunks of which he would've lost if he'd deferred.

When the time came to leave for Jerusalem, his parents and his younger sister drove all the way down from Boston to New York City to see him off. His father had pulled him aside in the airport terminal, and in a quiet, powerful moment unparalleled in their relationship, Avner told him how proud he was, and that nothing would make him happier than seeing Jonah surpass him as a rabbinical scholar. They'd embraced briefly, tightly, and when the plane broke the clouds and Jonah gazed out at the limitless blue sky, he knew he'd taken the first step on a journey that would change his life.

He wasn't wrong. He just hadn't expected the journey to

take a hard left turn.

And he certainly never imagined that his changed path would lead him so far away from the father in whose shadow he'd always walked.

He heard his mother's footsteps again, doubled this time by his father's heavier footfall. A second later his mom turned the corner with a smile, her husband close at her heels.

"Look what Jonah brought us." She swept her arm to indicate the table, but Avner Spellman's mouth remained in an even line.

"Good morning, Jonah," the rabbi said formally, taking a seat. Of medium height but with broad shoulders and a strong build, his dad had always been an imposing figure. Now, with his close-trimmed beard gone gray and his tortoiseshell frames worn pushed down the bridge of his nose, he looked every inch the erudite academician, squinting down at the frivolous world from the distant height of his ivory tower.

"Hey, Dad." Jonah forced ease into his voice as his mom settled into the last chair. "How've you been?"

"Busy. This is my first Hanukkah at Temple Sinai; it's important to set the appropriate tone."

"Of course," Jonah agreed, though he suspected they diverged on what constituted an appropriate tone for a joyous celebration of miraculous faith.

The three of them ate quietly for a few minutes, the

scrape of knives across bagels and the occasional slurp of coffee the only sounds in the hushed kitchen. Jonah shifted uncomfortably in his seat, searching for something to say, then grinned as he hit upon an idea.

"I had a funny coincidence last night. We got a call about an apartment fire in the Central West End. Wasn't too dramatic—the sprinkler system went off so it didn't spread beyond the kitchen—but I felt for the woman who lived in the apartment; she'd clearly been setting up a romantic dinner for someone when a piece of cardboard caught fire on the stove. She'd put candles out, nice table settings, and I even spotted—"

"So what was the coincidence?" his dad asked.

"Right. Well, it turned out she lives next door—or her sister does, I guess. I saw her later that night. You know my neighbor, Naomi? I didn't make the connection because they have different last names, but Eliana—"

"Oh, it was Ellie Bloom?" his mom asked, glancing up with slightly more interest.

"Ellie," he repeated, as though tasting the nickname. It suited her—though fancy, Eliana was too flowery and formal for the woman he'd met briefly last night. She'd been so gracious, resilient, even wryly joking despite the devastation in her blue eyes, he sensed that pretty, strawberry-blond exterior was the window dressing on a complex depth of spirit.

He hoped whoever she'd made that dinner for appreciated her value.

"Yes, Ellie Bloom," he said again, realizing his parents were watching him expectantly. "How do you know her?"

His mom waved a hand. "I don't, really—only by reputation. Her mom was Adele Bloom, and everyone says she was the queen of the Hanukkah performance. Someone was just telling me the other day about how the play was Adele's pride and joy, and that she managed to top herself every year, despite raising those two girls on her own. I can't remember who told me, let's see, was it before or after I went to the dentist on Wednesday? It must've been after, because I was—"

"What happened to Adele?" Jonah asked, eager to curtail one of his mother's detailed trips down recent-memory lane.

"Oh, she died. A couple years back. Cancer, I think. Her husband died, too, but a long time ago—when the girls were young, I believe."

"That's tough," he said, mostly to himself, sitting with the knowledge that the woman he'd met last night had faced much greater losses than an apartment's worth of sodden possessions. He took a moment to be grateful for his own parents, for their health and happiness and proximity. He may not always agree with them—in fact the gulf of differing opinion between him and his father could comfortably be described as gaping—but it was all petty by comparison.

"So now she's burned down her apartment cooking for her boyfriend?" his mom confirmed, clearly teeing up the gossip.

"As I understand it, yes."

"Poor thing. She sounds like a magnet for tragedy."

"Speaking of tragedy, we may have to cancel the Hanuk-kah performance this year. Mrs. Garber is immobilized with a back injury, and no one else has volunteered to take her place. Plenty of parents are willing to assist, but nobody wants to lead." Avner took a bite of a cream-cheese-laden bagel, his characteristically upright carriage making even that simple act seem solemn and of great importance.

Jonah stared at his father, a swell of irritation tightening his chest. "I told you I'd do it, about two minutes after you found out Mrs. Garber hurt her back. Remember?"

Avner blinked repeatedly behind his glasses, as if strug-gling to recall, but Jonah didn't buy it. His father was no fool, and he missed exactly nothing.

"You did mention something about the Hanukkah play," Avner said just as Jonah was opening his mouth to remind him again. "Maybe I misunderstood—I thought it was just an offer to help out, not to take on the whole thing. Surely you're too busy with work."

Jonah could swear he heard disdain as his father pro-nounced that last word. "It's no problem."

"But your shifts are so unpredictable. And of course the emergencies…"

Jonah gritted his teeth. His dad made no secret of his disappointment in his son's decision to abandon his ordination and train as a firefighter-EMT instead. Jonah was fine with that—well, he wasn't fine with it, but he'd been prepared for the series of confrontations that followed when he announced his choice to his parents.

This interminable, passive-aggressive, simmering tension, on the other hand, drove him up the wall. Avner had turned what should've been an explosive but contained argument into a war of attrition, and if Jonah was honest with himself, his dad was winning.

Jonah had only recently moved back to New York City from Israel and finished his firefighter-EMT training when his dad was offered the job at Temple Sinai. With no real ties to the city, Jonah figured it might shrink the emotional distance between him and his father if he also closed the physical distance. He thought following them to St. Louis would be a gesture of devotion so grand that his father couldn't possibly stay mad. Avner would accept Jonah's choice of career and they would revert to the loving father-and-son duo they'd always been.

Jonah couldn't have been more wrong.

He wasn't sure what about his presence so bothered his father. Was he a reminder of Avner's failure to deliver a scion to the Spellman rabbinical legacy? Was he embarrassed for his brand-new congregation to see that his eldest son had traipsed along behind his parents instead of leading a productive, independent life somewhere else?

Or had Jonah so disappointed him that his father simply

wanted nothing to do with him anymore?

"I'm on days for the next week, so it'll be fine."

Avner looked unconvinced, but he shrugged. "Up to you. I just hope it'll be a credit to Temple Sinai. Apparently the play attracts a lot of people who aren't regular attendees, so it could be a huge boost to our numbers—or it could remind a lot of them why they skip services in the first place. It's easy to write off Hanukkah as a holiday you can do at home, without going to shul. I'd love to show the audience that it can be even more meaningful to come to temple and celebrate with your community."

Jonah resisted the urge to roll his eyes. It was a kids' Hanukkah play, not Shakespeare—but if it was important to his father, it would be important to him, too. He needed a chance to show his dad that abandoning ordination didn't mean his commitment to his faith had wavered in the slightest. If anything, it was stronger than ever.

"It'll be great. I promise," Jonah said firmly.

Skepticism gleamed in his father's eyes, but the rabbi said nothing. His mother glanced between the two of them and tactfully changed the subject, but Jonah's resolve only stiffened as the minutes wore on.

If his dad wanted the best-ever Hanukkah play, he'd get one. And maybe—just maybe—the flames lined up in the menorah would be enough to begin melting the thick wall of ice that separated them.

Chapter Four

"SORRY, SORRY, SORRY." Ellie didn't glance up from her phone as she burst through the doors into the sanctuary, ten minutes late for the first rehearsal of the Hanukkah performance. Having to commute from her sister's house made her day feel shorter than usual, and although her boss was fine with her having to leave early to make this after-school rehearsal, he'd inevitably waved her off with a huge pile of work to finish before she came in the next morning.

"Let...me...just...send...this..." she said slowly, her hands flying over her phone's keyboard as she finished an email to her boss. She tapped the send button and finally looked up with a triumphant smile—then dropped her jaw halfway to the floor.

Instead of a loose group of kids milling around, waiting for their newly appointed director, they all stood in a neat little row at the front of the room—led ably by none other than Sexy Firefighter.

He smiled at her, a dazzling, knee-weakening display of white teeth and dimples and tiny eye-corner crinkles that nearly reduced her to a puddle of goo on the ground. Only sheer force of will and, to give credit where it's due, a skeleton held her upright.

Did he treasure last night's shared moment the way she did? All day she'd thought about the man in the window, joining her in an act of faith and celebration, a tradition transcending the panes of glass and cold winter air that separated them.

"Hi," she said brightly, sticking out her hand as they met halfway up the aisle. "Ellie Bloom."

"I remember. Jonah Spellman." His hand dwarfed hers, big and warm and strong, and she had to swallow hard before she could speak again.

"Nice to meet you properly, Jonah. My nephews have nothing but praise for their new Hebrew school teacher." She glanced past him at Gideon and Isaac, who waved eagerly.

"Glad to hear it. How's your apartment?"

"A mess. Luckily insurance will cover most of the costs, but it's going to take a long time to repair and replace everything."

He inclined his head sympathetically. "Water damage is a killer. I guess you'll be staying with your sister for a while?"

His tone as he asked the question was inscrutable. Was he eager for her to remain next door, perhaps so they could repeat what happened last night? Or was he wondering whether to move his menorah so he could light his candles with privacy?

"A couple of weeks at least," she replied—and could've

sworn he smiled a little wider.

"I guess we'll be neighbors a little longer, then. Did you come by to help with the Hanukkah performance?"

"Actually, I'm directing it," she replied, unable to keep the pride from her voice. It had been a long time since she'd stuck more than a toe in the theater world, and she felt ready to jump in headfirst.

Jonah's smile faltered. "Sorry, I think there's been a miscommunication. I'm directing the play this year."

She blinked up at him, sure she'd misheard. "Beg pardon?"

"Mrs. Garber hurt her back, so—"

"So I'm stepping in to fill her shoes."

"I spoke to my dad—I mean, Rabbi Spellman this morning and told him I'd do it."

"Well, I called him this afternoon, and he was delighted that I volunteered."

Jonah's expression darkened. "Was he."

"My mom directed the play for years. It makes sense for me to pick up the reins. But you're welcome to stay and help," she offered.

"Rabbi Spellman must be confused. He probably thought you'd be helping me."

"He really didn't," Ellie lobbed back, unable to keep the irritation from her tone. She didn't sprint out of the office and elbow her way through school dismissal traffic to argue with the rabbi's son—even if he was awfully nice to look at.

"I told him I would direct the play, he thanked me for volunteering. Your name—"

"Didn't come up. Of course." Jonah sighed, clearly exasperated, although Ellie didn't know why.

Shouldn't he be relieved? Wrangling ten—nope, she counted again, twelve—kids aged from kindergarten to fifth grade into a meaningful performance in less than a week was no easy task. Even she was a little daunted, but her determination to live up to her mom's legacy would see her through.

What was in it for him?

"You should work together," came a voice from the increasingly antsy line of children. She and Jonah turned in unison to see her five-year-old nephew Isaac looking at them expectantly.

"Aunt Ellie's the best at acting, Mr. Jonah is the best at Hebrew, so together you can make the best play," he said matter-of-factly.

The kids all nodded in agreement, and Ellie felt like she was being chided by a string of bobblehead dolls.

"What a wonderful idea. I would love to codirect with Mr. Jonah," she lied.

"Me, too," Jonah agreed, and she could tell from the tension in his jaw that his enthusiasm was exactly as insincere as hers.

"Perfect," Ellie muttered dryly. She looked at the kids getting wigglier by the minute, then at her brand-new codirector, his handsome face shadowed and preoccupied. In her bag she had a whole notebook of ideas she'd scribbled on her lunch hour, with printouts of pictures and costume concepts and set designs stuffed between its pages. She had a plan—a performance that would capture the joy and significance of the holiday, a rich, complex display of music and light and drama that would have the audience on their feet, probably in tears. It would be wonderful—it would be a masterpiece.

It would've made her mom proud.

Now she just had to get Sexy Firefighter on board. How hard could it be?

"THIS IS WAY too ambitious." Jonah tossed the stack of papers on the pew beside him.

Ellie exhaled loudly, making no attempt to hide her annoyance. They'd been working to combine their respective scripts for nearly an hour. The kids had abandoned them to play red rover in the lobby, their parents would be arriving soon to pick them up, and they hadn't rehearsed a thing—because at this point they still had nothing to rehearse.

"And yours is way too basic." Ellie held up his three-page script between her thumb and forefinger as though she could barely stand to touch it.

"This is not Broadway. These are kids. Not professional thespians."

"They're capable of way more than your simple script, and if we go ahead with mine, their parents won't be fuming that they rushed home from work to catch a ten-minute Hanukkah downer."

"My play is not a downer," he exclaimed, audibly shocked. "It's solemn. Sophisticated."

"It's almost entirely in Hebrew."

"And?"

"Not all Jewish people speak Hebrew, Jonah, especially not this fluently. I don't know what kind of temple you went to in…"

"Boston," he supplied.

"Boston," she repeated. "But Temple Sinai is a friendly, accessible, open-minded Reform community. It's not super formal, and the religious education reflects that. My Hebrew isn't this good and I grew up in this congregation, so I can't imagine—"

"Well, I think that's changing. You're right—there was no comprehensive language program when I arrived, and now one exists. Maybe it's time to rethink the Hanukkah play, too."

Ellie shook her head. "My mom did it this way for more than twenty years. A big, colorful, over-the-top production with lots of bells and whistles. Everyone loves it."

"No offense, Ellie, but I'm not sure you're still an expert on what this congregation wants. I've been here for six months and I've never seen you come to a service."

She dug her nails into her palms, feeling like she'd been slapped. He wasn't wrong.

It dawned on her that she hadn't been to shul since her mom died almost exactly two years earlier. At first it was too painful, too cutting to have to sit somewhere her mom loved without her, to see someone else sitting in her mom's favorite seat, to bear the weight of all the pitying glances, the patted hands, the well wishes.

That pain hadn't necessarily lessened, but she'd shifted it to the background and drowned it out with work. Accepted her sister's invitations, then bailed on the day with a quick text: *Stuck at work, happy Purim/Pesach/Rosh Hashanah!* Naomi hadn't even asked her if she was going to last year's Hanukkah performance; her absence had become a foregone conclusion.

"It's funny," she found herself saying aloud. "When I came in tonight, I hadn't even realized how long I'd been away. I guess this place still feels like home."

"It is your home, and it always will be." Jonah smiled for the first time in nearly an hour, before quickly reassuming his businesslike expression. "It's mine, too, now, and I think I'm a little more tapped in to what the kids' parents want."

"I don't have to be a weekly temple-goer to know that ten minutes of boring talking—seven minutes of which are in Hebrew—is not what anyone wants."

"And what qualifies you as the arbiter of Hanukkah play audience opinion?"

"As a matter of fact, I'm an actress," she said primly.

He narrowed his eyes. "You look like you just came from an office."

"Well, yes, I have a day job as an executive assistant at a bank, but I also have an agent and a short-term plan to move to Los Angeles. Very short term," she added, mostly for her own reassurance.

"Wonderful. In the immediate term, however—"

"We need to come up with a script, and yours simply won't work. Accept it and move on." She slammed his script upside down on the pew.

Jonah laughed incredulously. "Mine won't work? Mine is workable. Yours is a three-ring circus."

"Who doesn't love the circus?" she demanded, seconds before an enormous crash sounded from outside. They exchanged a look that promised they'd finish this later, then rushed out to the lobby.

"It was an accident," Gideon cried preemptively as they stepped into the lobby. Two of the older kids were trying to rehang a bulletin board on the nails from which it had evidently fallen, while the younger ones scurried around collecting the myriad bits of paper that had scattered all over the floor.

Jonah issued a series of firm commands in Hebrew that she didn't understand, but the kids did. They doubled the speed of their paper gathering and then wordlessly assembled into a straight line.

Jonah watched the two trying to fix the bulletin board, hands on his hips, then waved them away with a sigh. He heaved it up and pressed it against the wall, and Ellie rushed forward to help guide the hanging wire back onto the screws.

"That's one," she murmured. "Let me just..." She reached across him to the far edge, her arm between his chest and the board, her cheek dangerously close to his shoulder. She tried to ignore the heat of his body palpable through her blouse, the hint of strong, hard muscle as his biceps brushed against her rib cage, that he was so tall she had to push right onto her tiptoes to—

His scent hit her full force, like a bursting dam, and it was all she could do to stay on her feet. Clean, bright, and crisp; the architectural beauty of icicles clinging to tree branches; the cold burst of air into a too-warm room from a door flung open to a winter's night; a landscape of stars twinkling in a sky as dark and limitless as his eyes.

Eyes she belatedly realized were focused expectantly on her.

"All good?" Jonah asked.

She nodded, dropping her hands and backing away from him like he was on fire, when in fact all the heat in the lobby seemed to have relocated directly into her face.

"All good," she lied.

He finished securing the bulletin board, then looked over at the already wiggling line of kids.

"Today's rehearsal is a write-off. Let's have the kids run

through the Hanukkah blessings, then you and I can get together to finalize the script. What does your day look like tomorrow?"

"Not good." She opened her calendar on her phone and cringed. "Terrible. Could you meet me at my office downtown? Around lunchtime?"

"I'm on the day shift this week, but if everything's quiet, I might be able to sneak out for an hour."

They negotiated their respective schedules, finally making a plan for Jonah to come to her office at midday.

"All right, *kinder*. Back inside." He nodded the children back inside. Ellie followed, a mixture of admiration and resentment stirring in her gut.

He had such an easy way with the kids, authoritative yet familiar, whereas her absence from the temple meant she barely recognized all but a few of them, and none of them knew her by name.

More than ever, she wanted to reclaim her—and her mother's—place at Temple Sinai. But how could she with Jonah standing in her way?

THE REHEARSAL FINISHED as unproductively as it started, and Ellie drove Gideon and Isaac home. They lit the second night's candle in the menorah as a family, and after helping to bathe the boys Ellie found herself once again climbing the stairs later than planned, full of food and laughter and contentment.

She paused at her bedroom door before turning on the light. Across the gap separating the houses Jonah's window was dark. Had he lit his menorah earlier and it had already burned out?

Or was he waiting for her?

All day she'd kept last night's encounter carefully sectioned off in her mind. She hadn't mentioned it to anyone, and she and Jonah had also kept it secret, somehow mutually agreeing not to acknowledge it even to each other. The moment lived quite outside the overexposed reality of daytime; cloistered, hushed, it felt like a ritual that transcended the tawdriness of the day-to-day.

At least it did in Ellie's mind, which, to be fair, always had a flair for the dramatic. Jonah probably hadn't given it a second thought, chalked it up to an amusing coincidence, and moved on with his life.

She crossed the room with a sigh, only flipping on the small bedside lamp to keep the room dim. Yes, Jonah was attractive, and smart, and kind, and did she mention attractive? He was also stubborn and very much an obstacle to her vision for the Hanukkah play, so this was no time to construct a grand romantic fantasy out of one chance encounter. Tomorrow they'd reopen their United Nations–scale negotiations on the script, and she had to be firm and tough, not swooning over their secret nighttime connection.

With that in mind she marched to the sill and stuck her candles in their holders, sparing no time for elegance and keeping her eyes firmly on the task at hand. She struck the match, lit the shamash in the center of the menorah—and caved to her itching desire to glance at Jonah's window.

He was there.

Her breath caught in her throat as she made out his form in the darkness, faintly illuminated by his matching lit shamash candle. Like last night he lifted his hand in greeting, and she returned the gesture. In unison they began to murmur the blessing, using the shamash to light two candles this time, from left to right.

Ellie's mouth moved with the prayer but her mind raced in a different direction. Was this another coincidence? Had he waited for her? Would he want to talk about it tomorrow? What did this mean for their uneasy and certainly temporary truce about the script?

She moved her hand slowly, her thoughts calming as she repeated the familiar words. It didn't matter. Tomorrow would be tomorrow. This ritual of theirs was separate, sacred, a shared glimpse of light through thick black clouds. It didn't have to mean anything—or maybe it meant every-thing while it lasted. She would enjoy it for what it was—a mutual secret, an unspoken agreement, a brief but anchoring connection in what often felt like the freefall of her life.

She replaced the shamash and smiled up at Jonah. He smiled back, and for a moment neither of them moved, gazes locked, the distance between them feeling ever so slightly smaller than last night.

Then he inclined his head as if to say good-night. She did the same, moving away from the window to get ready for bed.

When she turned out the light a little while later, her candles had almost melted away, the flames riding on short stubs of wax. She slid between the sheets and watched them burn out, one by one, each flame flickering and faltering and finally extinguishing, a plume of smoke rising from the wick.

The last one went out, plunging the room into total darkness. She turned over in bed, closed her eyes, and fell into one of the best sleeps she'd had in a long time.

Chapter Five

JONAH TRIED THREE times before he found the right door to get to Ellie's office. The first led to the parking garage; the second opened into the ground-floor service center, which had tellers and ATMs but no access to the corporate office; and the third opened into an expansive, gleaming lobby with multiple banks of elevators constantly rocketing up and down the length of the gleaming skyscraper.

Eventually he found his way to some eye-wateringly high floor, where a friendly but intimidatingly well-dressed woman escorted him through a labyrinth of cubicles to the one Ellie occupied. She was on the phone but held up a finger to indicate she was almost ready.

He surveyed her workplace while he waited, marveling at the complex geometry of the cubicles and wondering who sat in the offices on the distant periphery. Important people, he supposed, doing important things necessitating the privacy of frosted glass.

"Absolutely. It'll be on your desk by three o'clock. Speak soon." Ellie hung up the phone, shot him a quick smile of greeting, threw a few things into her purse, and grabbed her coat off the back of her chair.

"Let's get out of here before anyone else asks me for a favor."

He followed her back through the maze and into the elevator, admiring the smooth way she cut a path through the crowded hallways. Ellie was petite, but she parted groups of people like the Red Sea.

"You mentioned yesterday you were an executive assistant. What exactly does that mean?" he asked once they'd reached the ground floor and found a table in the building's coffee shop.

"My boss tells me to jump and I ask how high." She rolled her eyes over the rim of her cardboard coffee cup.

"Seriously, what do you do all day? I've never seen a phone ring so much."

She smiled, a little bitterly. "That's because I actually pay attention whenever we have training, so lots of people who don't come to me for the information they never bothered to learn. Technically I should only be handling my boss's stuff—scheduling, prepping his files for meetings, proofreading documents—and using any downtime to step in and help with meatier tasks, things that might help me pivot out of this role and into more strategic project management. It's a great idea, except instead my downtime—and a good chunk of my uptime, come to think of it—is spent playing help desk to anyone with a question. Weird light blinking on the printer? Call Ellie. Not sure how to submit your vacation request? Call Ellie. Cut your finger while you were slicing a bagel and need a Band-Aid, oh and also how do you fill in an incident report, and by the way where are cleaning products stored because there's blood all over the staff kitchen?"

"Call Ellie," he supplied.

"Bingo."

"I'm stressed just listening, never mind actually doing your job. Give me a burning building over a printer light any day."

"The blinking green lights are fine; the solid reds are the ones that make me wish I'd also chosen a more dangerous profession."

As if on cue, her cell phone rang. She apologized as she picked it up, listened for a moment, and then delivered what struck him as a highly technical but clear, concise set of instructions for some sort of complex engineering issue. Jonah leaned in, listening carefully, trying to understand what she was explaining. Was it a critical outage? Maybe a building-wide malfunction? The person on the other end seemed frantic.

Suddenly the caller shouted "Eureka" so loudly he could hear it over the din of the café. Ellie ended the call and put her phone facedown on the table.

"He couldn't work the coffee machine. Sorry, where were we?"

"Your incredibly difficult job. I have to say, you seem extraordinarily good at it."

"I am. Terrific, in fact. Too bad I hate every second I'm here."

"Then why do it?"

"Money. Before my mom got sick, I was trying to make it as an actress—a couple of commercials here and there, a few promising auditions—and working with some of the elementary schools in Clayton on their drama programs. I wasn't earning a lot, but I got by. My mom was my biggest fan. When I was a kid, she even took me to a local casting call for a movie, and I got the part. Did you ever see *Jessica Bookworm*? It's super old now, but it was about a girl who—"

"Sort of manifests everything she reads into reality?"

"That's the one."

"You were in that?"

"In a supporting but critical role as Jessica's loyal friend, Frances. I was in three scenes, but it felt like a big deal. It was filmed locally, with real Hollywood talent. My mom was over the moon—she was convinced I was on my way to an Academy Award and no one could tell her otherwise. Anyway, she supported me ever since. Then, about three years ago, she was diagnosed with lymphoma."

He winced. "That's tough."

"It was a blow," she agreed. "My dad passed away very suddenly from an aneurysm when I was in middle school—days before the *Jessica Bookworm* premiere in Los Angeles, actually, so in the end I couldn't go. It was just the three of us—me, my mom, and my sister—for a long time. Most of my mom's savings went into putting Naomi and me through college, and the bills added up quickly. Naomi had two kids at home to support, so it made sense for me to try to boost my income. At the time, getting this job felt like an enormous blessing."

"When did your mom die?"

"Almost two years ago exactly. Just after Hanukkah."

"Yehi zichra baruch."

She smiled. "Thank you. This is a hard time of year."

He inclined his head in acknowledgment, and then they both sipped their coffee in silence, allowing the moment to run its course.

"So why stay in a job you hate once the medical bills stopped increasing?" he asked eventually.

"Same reason—money. Only now it's for me. Once I've saved up enough, I'm moving to Los Angeles to really give my acting career a shot, just like my mom always wanted. I'm nearly there. The apartment fire was a setback, but I'm hoping my end-of-year bonus will make up most of the shortfall."

"Los Angeles," he echoed, feeling oddly disappointed that she wouldn't be in his orbit much longer. It shouldn't make any difference to him—he barely knew her, and even their fun, secret nightly ritual had an impending time limit. Plus she probably found their mirrored menorah lighting novel rather than meaningful.

"How does your boyfriend feel about that?" he tossed

out, trying to sound casual.

She frowned at him for a second, her expression quizzical, then she burst into laughter. "I guess you spotted the charred remains of my romantic dinner for two. I was cooking for a guy I was sort-of seeing—Jeff. He called to break up with me, and then everything went up in flames. Poetic, really."

"I hope he at least bought you a replacement tea towel as an apology."

"He doesn't even know about the fire. It's fine—I wasn't that into him. In retrospect he was one more excuse not to pick up and leave, so I guess he did me a favor. Now there's nothing tying me here."

Jonah nodded, swallowing his disappointment. Clearly he'd been single too long—he was seeing possibilities where they didn't exist. No point in imagining a connection that was almost definitely unreciprocated. That was a short, sure road to heartbreak.

"Well, we're lucky to have you before you hit it big. Don't forget to mention the Temple Sinai Hanukkah play in your Oscar speech."

"Are you kidding? I'll be thanking the brave firefighter who looked death square in the eye as he pulled me from a burning building."

He laughed. "That's not quite how I remember it, but I'll take the credit."

"You deserve it. You have such a cool job. Did you always want to be a firefighter?"

He shook his head, always feeling a little sheepish about this admission. "I've only been doing this for the last year or so. Before that I was studying to be ordained as a rabbi."

Her brows shot up. "Wow. That is quite the pivot. Are you taking a break from rabbinical school or are you—"

"Done," he said firmly. "It wasn't the right path for me."

"Well, good for you for figuring that out before you wasted too much time doing something you're not passionate about. A lesson I should've learned a while back."

"It wasn't easy, but it was the correct choice." He shifted in his seat, uncomfortable with the direction this conversation had taken. "I know you've got to get back to work, so maybe we should jump into the script."

"Absolutely. Did you see the version I sent over this morning?"

"I did," he said as they simultaneously pulled out two printed, stapled copies, each having made an extra for the other.

They shared a quick, collegial smile across the table, and then Ellie pulled out a red pen, all business.

"I tried to incorporate the best parts of both our efforts. Admittedly yours had some of the gravity and solemnity mine lacked, and it was certainly more streamlined and easier to pull together in a handful of days. Mine, however, had way more pizzazz. What I ended up with is hopefully both educational, fun, and most importantly, doable given our limited time."

"Your version is very good," he agreed. "However there are key ways in which mine is better."

After twenty minutes and a negotiation so complicated it would make a top-ranking diplomat's eyes cross, they had a revised script they were both *almost* happy with.

"Don't they say you know it's a good compromise when both parties are a little disgruntled when they leave the table?" Jonah picked up his coffee cup for a sip but put it down with a grimace. He'd been so focused on their discussion, he'd let it go cold.

"I've never heard that," she grumbled, but put the cap on her red pen and dropped it into her purse.

He picked up his cup. "Can I get you another? I was so engrossed in debating whether King Antiochus needed a crown *and* a scepter that I forgot to caffeinate."

"Thank goodness. Not sure I could've triumphed quite so handily if you'd been firing on all cylinders."

"*Triumph* isn't the word I'd use. Another latte?"

She shook her head. "I'd love to—and not just because I think with more time I could grind down your resistance to pyrotechnics. But I have to get back upstairs and attend to the"—she turned her phone over for the first time since she'd solved the coffee-machine crisis—"seventeen missed calls from people who aren't my boss."

"Fair enough." He put his cup down.

"I'll see you tonight at…" She trailed off as he shook his

head, then snapped her fingers in realization. "Of course. Shabbat. No rehearsal."

"But we do have rehearsal tomorrow night."

"I'll be there. Meanwhile my sister and I are going prop shopping before dinner this evening, so text me if you think of anything we need." She smiled brightly.

"Will do."

They both stood, and he gathered their two cardboard cups to toss in the trash. "Thanks for taking the time out of your day to fix the script. I hope it didn't set you too far back with everything else you've got going on."

She flicked her wrist. "Please, I should thank you for giving me an excuse to disappear for a while. Who knows, maybe I'll return to discover that in my absence, someone made the effort to read the user manual for their office laptop."

Her phone rang in her hand.

"Or not." She sighed. "Either way, this was probably the most productive meeting I've had this week. Thank you."

"Thank *you*," he echoed as they made their way out of the coffee shop and back to the bank of elevators. "I wasn't exactly gracious when you stepped in to help with the Hanukkah play. I spent so long learning how to lead from the front, sometimes I forget that it's okay to walk beside someone, too."

Her gaze met his and lingered, and the corners of her lips tilted up. Warmth stirred in his heart, reminding him for the first time in a while that it still existed. He hadn't dated anyone seriously since college, at first too lost in the elevated labyrinths of theology and philosophy to waste time on earthly pursuits like romance, and then too busy charting a new course through life, too focused on recalibrating his future to give much thought at all to the here and now—including the woman standing right in front of him.

Ellie had a lovely smile.

And an imminent plan to move to Los Angeles.

He took a half step back, remembering the romantic scene that had been spoiled by the fire, reminding himself of all the pressures and disappointments she was on the brink of escaping. Even if his interest was reciprocated, he had no business complicating her life. He barely had his own figured out.

They would just be friends.

And cocreators of the world's best Hanukkah play, of course.

"Have a good Shabbos, and I'll see you tomorrow." He lifted a hand in a stiff farewell.

"You, too."

Neither of them moved. They stood still, as if they might become pillars of salt if they turned away, lingering in this brief respite from the day's more serious and insistent demands, reluctant to step out of their easy accord and back into the tumult.

Ellie's phone rang.

She groaned, audibly exasperated, and he rocked on his heels, snapping back to reality so quickly he rolled his neck, checking for whiplash.

Pillars of salt? What the hell, Spellman? You can take the boy out of seminary...

"I really have to go," Ellie said apologetically, already backing toward the elevators. "We'll talk later, okay?"

"No problem. Have a good rest of your day."

She shot him a grateful look, then answered the phone, turning her back on him fully as she hurried toward the elevator. She slipped through the gap in an already closing door and just like that, she was gone.

Jonah exhaled for what felt like the first time in an hour. The warmth that prompted a momentary thaw in his heart rode out on two lungs' worth of breath, replaced by the crisp, wintry air that blew through the constantly swinging door in the lobby. The cold rushed through his skull and he blinked repeatedly, feeling like a big chunk of frost had just fallen off a window and he suddenly had a clear view.

Ellie was a nice woman—a nice woman who was not interested in him, and who already had this town in her rearview mirror. He, on the other hand, was still laying the foundation of a life here, trying to make it strong enough to support everything he wanted, not to mention sufficiently tough to survive the battering it would take as he rebuilt his relationship with his father.

Their paths would intersect for eight nights, then diverge

forever.

He swung around and started toward the exit, hands in his pockets. Maybe that was part of the gift of the holiday—knowing it would come to an end, so enjoying it while it lasted.

At least they had a few nights left before their connection would be extinguished, just like the candles in their windows.

Chapter Six

E LLIE DIDN'T BOTHER glancing at the time on her phone as she race-walked up the sidewalk as fast as her pencil skirt would allow. She could tell from her sister's face that she was obnoxiously late, as usual.

"Sorry, sorry, sorry," she began before she reached Naomi, who shook her head dismissively.

"It's fine. Dan has the boys, but we need to be quick so we don't throw off the whole dinner-and-bedtime routine."

"Of course. This'll be the fastest Hanukkah play prop purchase ever recorded."

Naomi started to push open the door of Second Chance, the antiques store on Orchard Hill's suburban version of a main drag, then paused, squinting at the sign hanging on the ornamental glass. "It might have to be—the shop closes in fifteen minutes."

Ellie swore under her breath as she followed Naomi inside. The hour she'd taken out of her workday to meet Jonah for coffee really shouldn't have derailed her entire afternoon—but given everyone expected her to be at their beck and call, inevitably it had. When she finally finished wading through all the "one quick questions" that piled up in her absence and got down to her actual to-do list, the day was nearly over and she wanted to scream in frustration.

Instead she gritted her teeth, took a deep breath, and thought about California.

She'd never been, but in her mind's eye it was beautiful. Bright, warm, full of palm trees and iced coffees and friendly people with sun-bleached highlights and perfect white teeth. The complete opposite of dull, cold Eastern Missouri, a place that had once given her so much joy—and then snatched it all back.

"This place is stunning," Naomi breathed, prompting Ellie to look around—and gasp at what she discovered.

Gone was the musty-smelling, disorganized thrift store parading as an antiques shop that had supplied all manner of weird and wonderful props during her days as a budding thespian. A new owner had taken over the space a few months earlier and, evidently, completely transformed the business.

The overstuffed clothing racks, haphazardly placed pieces of furniture and bursting cardboard boxes had been replaced by elegance and intention, wrapped in a festive decorative bow. The overhead lighting was low, but the shop sparkled, lit by what felt like thousands of tiny bulbs strung from the rafters, wrapped around columns, and draped over tables. Whereas the previous owner's pack-a-day habit meant the interior always smelled vaguely of cigarettes, now a series of strategically placed wax warmers filled the air with scents of cinnamon and vanilla so vivid Ellie's mouth watered as she inhaled.

"What happened here?" she mused aloud, turning in a circle to take in the array of inventory. Instead of odd stacks of mismatched china and heaped piles of costume jewelry, the shop boasted classy, curated pieces that could quite accurately be referred to as treasures. Beautiful vintage clothes in mint condition. Arresting, intriguing artwork, including a black-and-white series by a well-known local photographer. A limited but high-quality selection of antique furniture, including a roll-top desk that Ellie couldn't resist running a coveting palm across.

"I'm not sure we've come to the right place," Naomi murmured, and Ellie instantly took her meaning. Everything in the shop was gorgeous, but they were here to pick cheap cast-offs that could be repurposed into costumes and props—not redecorate a seven-bedroom mansion.

"Can I help you ladies find anything?"

Simultaneously the sisters turned toward the woman walking out from behind the till. She was dark-haired and willowy, with a friendly smile.

Ellie and Naomi exchanged a quick glance, and then Ellie said, "We love what you've done with the space. We used to come here every year to buy props for the Temple Sinai Hanukkah play. I think we might be priced out on that point, but we'll definitely be back. This store is amazing."

The woman crossed her palms over her heart. "Thank you so much! I won't lie, it took a lot of work, and I wasn't sure everyone would be happy to see the thrift shop go. Sounds like it was a beloved main-street fixture for a long time."

"A fixture, yes, beloved, maybe not quite. I'm Naomi, by the way, and this is my sister, Ellie." Naomi stepped forward and shook the woman's hand, and Ellie followed her lead.

"Noa Jacob."

"Nice to meet you, Noa," Ellie said warmly. "I know you're about to close up for the night, so we won't keep you, but I promise to find an excuse to come back as soon as I can."

Noa shook her head. "Don't be silly. I wanted to give Second Chance a makeover, for sure, but I don't want to erase its history. You came every year for props, and I'm not letting you leave without them."

Naomi raised a skeptical brow, glancing at the price tag on an ornate, gilded clock hanging on the wall beside them. "That's very kind, but I don't see how—"

"Follow me." With a mischievous smile, Noa quickly turned the sign on the door to read *Closed*, and then beckoned them toward the back of the store.

She led them through a door into the storage area at the back of the building, past a small office and staff kitchen area, then she opened another door and flicked on the light. Ellie stood rooted to the spot, gaping as she processed the view in front of her.

Evidently the previous owner hadn't taken all the old inventory—or any of it, from the looks of things. Boxes were stacked nearly to the ceiling, a veritable mountain of random objects, ready to unleash an avalanche of junk no one wanted to buy.

"Have at it," Noa told them with a flourish.

"Do you have…prices?" Naomi asked slowly, staring in disbelief.

"How about free?"

Now Ellie turned her incredulity toward Noa. "Seriously? We can just take stuff?"

"You'd be doing me a favor. And if you happen to unearth a priceless antique, you can keep it."

"Are you sure?" Naomi asked.

Noa smiled playfully. "It's a risk I'm willing to take."

Noa left them to it, calling breezily that she'd be out front if they needed anything. Alone in the box-filled room, Ellie and Naomi stood in bewildered silence for a moment before Naomi pulled a piece of paper from her purse.

"Bedtime waits for no one, so we better get started. First thing on the list: a crown for King Antiochus."

"And a scepter," Ellie added with a secretive smile, remembering her negotiation with Jonah earlier that day.

They reviewed the entire list so they knew what to be on the lookout for, then methodically began to work their way through the boxes, setting aside anything that might come in handy.

As they progressed and the piles of possibilities grew, the vision for the tone and palette of the play began to emerge, which would prompt the piles to shrink once more. Ellie would pull out two articles of clothing that could be repurposed into Maccabee costumes and set them aside, then find another piece that would be perfect for the background and, realizing it complemented one of the pieces of clothing much better than the other, would put the now-mismatched option in a box they'd designated so they didn't look at anything twice.

They didn't talk much—they didn't need to. They'd been through this process every year when their mom directed the Hanukkah play.

Every year until she died, Ellie mentally corrected.

She snuck a glance at her sister. Growing up they were inseparable, Ellie precocious and flamboyant, Naomi sweet and earnest, so different and yet more like each other than anyone else in the world.

They'd always been close, but after their father died it became about survival as much as entertainment. Their extended families were little more than collections of strangers, scattered all around the country, unfamiliar smiles at the funeral, disembodied voices on the phone. Their mom was neck-deep in grief and stress and fear, and so they clung to each other like they never had before, arms and hearts entwined no matter how much distance separated them.

When had they let go?

"Remember when we used to do this with Mom?" Naomi asked softly.

Ellie looked down at the purple, faux-velvet jumpsuit she intended to turn into the king's robe. Their mom would've loved it—so silly, yet so joyful.

"I do."

"Mrs. Garber is a lovely woman and she worked so hard on the play, but she never quite had Mom's…"

"Joie de vivre?"

"Exactly."

Naomi examined a sequined beret, then smiled over at her. "Mom would be so happy you're directing the Hanukkah play."

Ellie wrinkled her nose, telling herself her distaste was for the moldy smell of the leather purse she'd picked up. "I don't know. I think she might be disappointed I hadn't made more of myself by this point."

"Ellie," her sister chided sternly. "What are you talking about? You earn a great salary, you live in a chic apartment—"

"Which I burned down."

"Which will be restored to its previous glory, you just got a real-life Hollywood agent, and by this time next year you'll be living the dream in Los Angeles, maybe already on your way to mega stardom. You know Mom basically mapped out where your star would be on the Walk of Fame the first time you had a speaking part in the Hanukkah play. I can't imagine what she'd make of how far you've come, but I'm confident disappointment would have nothing to do with it."

Ellie shrugged, wishing she could believe her sister. "Sure, when you put it like that, it sounds great. Except so much of it hasn't happened yet. Monday morning I'll have to slog into work and spend nine hours doing annoying things for a company I don't care about."

"No one loves their job all the time," Naomi said, sounding exasperated.

"Well, I want to," Ellie muttered.

She bet Jonah did.

Her heartbeat stuttered at the thought of him, but she ignored it, choosing to focus on setting her sister straight.

"You know Mom wouldn't be impressed by money or a fancy zip code or a skyscraper downtown. She valued creativity, service, and personal fulfilment above anything else. That's why she was so proud when you became a social worker, and always encouraged me to follow my dream of a career in theater, no matter how steep the odds of success. I think she'd be sad that I've wasted so much time at the bank. She'd rather I was penniless but happy doing amateur theater in Los Angeles than miserable and well-paid in an office job."

Ellie stared pointedly at her sister, waiting for her to disagree, itching for the chance to justify out loud the decision she'd long suspected Naomi disapproved of.

But true to character, Naomi said nothing, didn't even glance up from the ceramic vase in her lap. Her younger sister had always been so good at disengaging, at simply stepping back from the conflicts Ellie tended to run into headlong. Although it infuriated her to no end, Ellie had always grudgingly respected that quality.

They sorted in silence for a little while longer, their recent accord giving way to the tension that had simmered between them since their mom died.

Ellie could never pinpoint the exact moment their once tightly clasped hands had dropped, but their relationship definitely deteriorated after she took the job at the bank. Naomi never argued—she and Dan agreed the money she earned was welcome and very much needed—but Ellie's longer work hours had meant the responsibility for caring for their mom fell more on Naomi's shoulders. With two children already, maybe her sister felt that burden was disproportionate. But then, who would've paid for the hospital bills? The appointments with specialists? The funeral?

Perhaps the gulf came afterward, when Naomi and Dan seemed to expect that Ellie would return to her patchwork income of teaching acting lessons, the odd workshop for the local school, the occasional paid part in a commercial or a local theater production. Only by then Ellie's outlook had changed. She didn't want to subsist and wait for her big break—she wanted to chase it, hunt it down, grab it with both hands.

She worked harder. Got promoted. Worked longer. Got a pay rise. Watched the zeroes pile up in her bank account, each one another hole in the wall separating her from her new life in Los Angeles.

Now that wall was so punctured she could practically step right through it—and her sister's dissatisfaction loomed larger than ever.

What was wrong with going after what she wanted, what she'd always dreamed about, what her mom had fully believed she could achieve? Naomi didn't get it—she was passionate about her career, loved her husband, thrived as mother, had a house and a family and a future beautifully mapped out. Ellie had nothing here. No boyfriend, no professional ties—she'd even drifted away from Temple Sinai. Why couldn't Naomi understand that it was her turn to find happiness? What else did she expect Ellie to do?

Ellie swallowed a sudden lump in her throat, blinking fiercely against unwelcome tears. Everything ended. People quit jobs, left cities. Parents died.

Maybe sisterhood had an expiration date, too.

Ellie flexed her fingers, knowing for sure her sister's hand was out of reach.

"Mom's anniversary is coming up," Naomi said quietly.

"I know," Ellie snapped, regretting her tone the instant she heard it. She added more gently, "It's on Tuesday."

"I thought I'd stop at the kosher grocery store on the way

home to get a yahrzeit candle. Do you want to come? We've got pretty much everything we need here."

Ellie smiled sadly at the cautious hope in her sister's voice. Once she would've immediately said yes, back when time was one of her most abundant resources, second only to the easy, seamless closeness of her family.

Everything was different now. Busier, sure, and also more widely set apart. She was grateful to be her sister's houseguest, and those first few days were fun, but the cracks were showing, ripping open the initial veneer of simplicity and comfort, too wide and jagged to be papered over by a couple of bottles of wine over dinner in the wake of a hilarious catastrophe.

"I wish I could. I had a crazy day today. I took an hour out to meet with Jonah to talk about the script for the play and it threw off my whole schedule. I need to rush home and log on to my laptop. I have a big document due first thing tomorrow morning. But I can get dinner started if that would help," she said, cringing at how obvious an after-thought it was.

Naomi shook her head, tossing a couple of final picks onto the pile and rising from the floor, dusting off her jeans. "You go ahead. I'll load all this into the car."

"I'll give you a hand."

"You've got work to do. I want to talk to Noa, anyway, about some of the stuff I saw up front. Go on home. I'd rather you got through enough work to join us for dinner."

"If you're sure," Ellie said hesitantly, already knowing there was virtually no chance she'd be eating anywhere other than on the tiny table in the guest room, in front of her laptop.

"I'm sure. I'll see you at home." Naomi smiled, so sincerely, but with that melancholy, rueful tug Ellie had never seen before their mom died, and now appeared in almost every conversation they had.

Ellie brushed off her hands and popped to her feet. Naomi told her to go—she'd go. She didn't have to apologize for having a hectic job—especially since it had kept them all afloat financially—and she didn't have to feel bad that sometimes it took precedence over spending time with her family.

So why did she feel so bad about it?

"Later, then," Ellie told her sister brightly. She left the room before Naomi could respond, breezed through the shop with a lifted hand before Noa could snag her in conversation, hurried down the sidewalk before anyone could see her face momentarily crumple, hear her breath hitch, or sense her brittle heart shatter into ten thousand pieces before she pulled it all back together.

She kept walking, head high, eyes clear, smile ready, her heart mangled and bleeding but still beating—just about.

Chapter Seven

"I LOVE WHAT you did with that, Zach. I could really feel your energy—your desire to overthrow the king. Let's try it one more time, and I want you to sink into the role a little more. Don't be afraid to go deep. Drop into that rage, that sense of injustice, that fired-up urge to make things right. Okay?"

Jonah hid his smile behind his hand as he watched ten-year-old Zach blink up at Ellie, doing his best to understand what she'd just told him but clearly bewildered.

"Okay," he said uncertainly.

"Fantastic. Let's take it from your line."

Zach held his makeshift sword aloft—at the moment it was just a long, cardboard rectangle—and paused before he delivered his line, perhaps trying to *sink in* as Ellie suggested.

He took a deep breath, furrowed his brow behind his glasses, and with what could fairly be described as burning conviction commanded, "Let's go!"

He and Ellie applauded in unison, and Zach lowered his sword with a smile.

"Was that better?" he asked eagerly.

Ellie put her palm over her heart. "I got chills."

Zach grinned, and Jonah rose from his seat in the front-row pew.

"I think we're set on the Maccabees' decision to rise up against King Antiochus. Should we move on to the restoration of the Temple?"

"Perfect." Ellie smiled over at him from where she stood by the edge of the raised platform at the front of the sanctuary. They'd only known each other a few days, but every time she looked at him like that—like she knew exactly what he was thinking, and bet he knew what was on her mind, too—it seemed they'd been friends for years.

Is that what they were—friends? Didn't feel like it. He couldn't put his finger on what exactly they were, but friends definitely wasn't sufficient.

Last night they'd lit the candles again, three this time, arriving at their windows within seconds of each other, as if tugged together like two thirsty cranes drawn to the nighttime glimmer of a whispering, freshwater stream.

They communicated more easily, if still silently, meeting each other's eyes across the space between the houses, smiling readily, waving goodbye when the full complement of candles was lit. No awkwardness, no ambiguity, at least not on his part, even though neither of them had ever acknowledged their nightly ritual out loud.

Their shared secret. He wondered if she was thinking about it right now, just as he was, as their gazes met and held and then broke apart.

He flipped through the pages in his script to the right one as Ellie herded Temple Restorers number one through five up onto the platform and showed each of them where to stand. He and Ellie agreed that every one of their pint-sized thespians should have a speaking part, and they'd predominantly designated their littlest participants as Temple Restorers, so they could keep busy sweeping and tidying in the background when not delivering their brief lines.

"How does that look?" Ellie asked him from the platform.

He assessed the children's positioning, then gave her a thumbs-up.

"Okay, *kinder*. Everyone have their line ready?"

They all held up the half sheets of paper they'd been given with their individual sentence printed on it—longer for the older ones, just a few words for the youngest.

"Ellie's got you standing in speaking order. Elisa, you're first. Then Isaac, Sara, Sonia, and finally David. Elisa, why don't you—"

The door at the back of the room creaked open, the kids standing up a little straighter as they stared past Jonah at the visitor. He glanced over his shoulder, his jaw tightening when he saw who'd joined them.

His father.

"Don't mind me." Rabbi Spellman waved them on with a smile, walking down the aisle to take a seat at the edge of the fourth row. "I've heard so much about the wonderful work you children are doing, I had to get a sneak preview. Pretend I'm not here."

His expression was warm and kindly, and the children were visibly reassured by his presence, but Jonah knew better. His dad had no concerns about the performers, but he would readily critique the play's erstwhile directors.

He snuck a look at Ellie, but she had already returned her attention to the children with an encouraging nod. She didn't seem worried in the slightest.

She didn't know his dad.

His father's gaze seemed to burn into his back as he guided the kids through the scene, twin beams harshly illuminating every doubt Jonah had about their raggedy production. Would the rabbi think the play lacked solemnity? Didn't challenge the kids enough? Challenged them too much? Jonah gritted his teeth, regretting his capitulation on how much of the script was in Hebrew. These kids were Hebrew students, after all—shouldn't they be showing off what they've learned?

"Look, I found a tiny jar of oil!" David proclaimed, holding aloft a squat, empty glass jar that had not yet been relieved of its salsa label.

Ellie burst into applause, and Jonah heard his dad join in. For the first time since the scene began he dared to turn around—and froze when he spotted a copy of the script draped over the rabbi's lap.

"Wonderful job," the rabbi said heartily. "I had no idea we had such gifted actors and actresses among us."

"Great work, Temple Restorers. I want you to sit in this same order and practice your lines again, okay?" She looked at another group of older children waiting in a pew. "Menorah lighters, you're up."

Rabbi Spellman eased up from his seat, flipping through the pages of the script as he approached Ellie, motioning for Jonah to join them.

Jonah's shoulders tensed as he took his place beside his father.

Here it comes.

"I'm so grateful you stepped up to direct the play, Ellie," he began, his gray beard framing an approving smile. When was the last time he'd smiled at his own son that way? Not since Jonah left for Israel.

"Your mother's reputation precedes you," Rabbi Spellman added, and Ellie ducked her head demurely.

"I'll never quite fill her shoes, but I'm happy for the chance to try them on for size."

"I think one of the kids left their script on the floor, so I had a quick read-through. I'm so impressed with what you were able to pull together in such a short time. Really, this is fantastic stuff."

"Thank you," Ellie replied warmly, but Jonah saw her gaze dart curiously in his direction. So she'd also noticed that his dad acted like he wasn't there—it wasn't all in his imagination.

"Can I offer just one suggestion? And that's all it is—this is your project, and I don't want to step on your toes."

"Of course. We'd welcome your feedback," Ellie said, smiling pointedly at Jonah before returning her attention to the rabbi.

If Rabbi Spellman noticed, he gave no sign. "Again, I think you've done so well. It's just—the Hebrew. There's an awful lot. Of course I'm proud that our children are developing such fluency, but I worry about alienating the parents and visitors who come to see the play. Perhaps we could highlight their proficiency in the language in a way that doesn't impede any non-Hebrew speakers' understanding of the plot?"

Jonah shifted his weight, bracing himself for defeat. He wouldn't blame Ellie for informing his father that the Hebrew was all his idea, and that she'd already fought to reduce it to the current amount. She wanted to make a good impression, too—what did she care if it came at his expense?

"That's an interesting point. Jonah is such a great teacher that all of the kids are desperate to show off their Hebrew ability. But we'll work on a way to make sure no one's missing out on the story. Right, Jonah?"

He could've kissed her. His heartbeat surged into double time, and his body itched with the urge to sweep her against his chest and press his mouth to hers in a long, thirsty, grateful kiss.

Instead he nodded tightly. "Definitely."

Rabbi Spellman looked at him as if he'd only just realized he was there, blinking behind his glasses. "Good."

"One other thing," the rabbi said, his tone sharpening as he solely addressed his son. "I want to make sure we're not putting any of these children under too much pressure. I see you've given every one of them a speaking part—I assume this is intentional?"

"We're emphasizing that the Hanukkah story is about the importance of the collective, not just a miracle. That true community is comprised of a million tiny actions—that the youngest contributor is no less significant than the oldest or most powerful."

"Beautifully put," Ellie remarked, but Rabbi Spellman frowned.

"Big ambitions for grade-school performers. Fine if you can pull it off, but the goal for them is to have fun and be proud of what they create. If any one of them is nervous or hesitant about speaking in front of an audience, I don't want you forcing them to do it."

Jonah's jaw tightened in annoyance. "I would never force a child to—"

"Ellie, I trust you'll keep Jonah reined in? He's never lacked for big ideas, but he struggles with execution."

Rabbi Spellman's tone was affectionately chiding, but each word was a barb lodged in Jonah's flesh. Clearly a Hanukkah détente was not on the cards this year—still,

Jonah hadn't expected to be so baldly undermined in public.

"To be honest, Rabbi, Jonah's been the one pumping the brakes on this production. To say my enthusiasm runs away with me is an understatement. Without his restraint, I'd probably be on the phone to the zoo trying to rent a bunch of camels."

If Jonah wanted to kiss Ellie before, now he would've happily dropped to one knee and pledged to be at her beck and call forever. Not only had she defended him, she did it with such a self-effacing, innocent smile, there was no way his father could possibly argue.

"I don't think our insurance covers wild animals," Rabbi Spellman joked, but Jonah didn't miss the fleeting, icy glare his father threw his way.

Don't screw this up, it warned.

"No camels, I promise." Ellie grinned.

"I'll leave you to it, then. Thanks for letting me drop in." Rabbi Spellman was back in diplomatic mode, returning Ellie's smile as he handed over the spare script. He complimented her again, shot a parting, skeptical look at Jonah, and then made his way back up the aisle and out of the sanctuary.

Ellie turned to him, a quizzical look on her face, but before either of them could speak one of the Menorah Lighters called from the platform.

"Ms. Ellie, Mr. Jonah, we're ready."

Jonah took in the line of increasingly antsy kids lined up

on the stage.

"Let's talk later," he told Ellie briskly.

"All right."

He walked back to his place in the front pew, all too aware that Ellie watched every step he took.

ELLIE WAVED OFF the last of the parents' cars as it pulled out of the parking lot, then shut the door and locked it from the inside as Rabbi Spellman instructed. Since it was a Saturday they'd had a midafternoon rehearsal, and the rabbi would be back that evening for the nightly Hanukkah candle-lighting. For now, though, the place was empty, and as she walked back through the lobby to the storage room off the sanctuary her footsteps echoed, the halls already dim as the weak, short-lived winter daylight gave way to darkness outside.

Jonah was stacking the boxes of props and she paused, leaning against the doorframe, admiring the long lines of his strong, lean body. He'd taken off his pullover, and she could see the play of muscle in his back through his thin T-shirt, the hard contours of his arms shadowed and enticing in short sleeves.

Jonah intrigued her to no end, making her simultaneously impatient and self-restrained. He was like a book so compelling she was desperate to peek at the last page to find out what happened, but at the same time she savored each line, each turn of phrase, not wanting it to be over too soon.

He was such a natural leader, commanding the kids' respect while being easygoing and accessible, a trusted friend as much as an instructor. It made sense that he'd considered ordination—he was smart and scholarly, yet had a sincere interest in people and teaching and improving the community around him.

So why had he quit? He didn't seem like the type not to finish something he'd started. Maybe something happened—or maybe it really was like he'd said, that he just didn't feel it was the right path.

Then there was his dad, and the dynamic between them—so frosty she'd practically felt her hair freezing into icicles. Her own interactions with Rabbi Spellman were a world apart; she'd found him friendly, encouraging, and grateful for volunteers of any ability. But when he spoke to his son, his disapproval loomed like a shadow, and when Jonah spoke to him, the words practically crackled with hostility.

They seemed like two reasonable, intelligent men. What happened to put them at such palpable and irreconcilable odds?

Jonah hefted up the box and she straightened, giving herself a mental shake. She had no business thinking about him this way, like they could be anything other than passing acquaintances. He had just moved here—she was on her way out for good. Jeff had been her last-ditch attempt at dating, which had literally gone up in flames. She absolutely did not need the distraction of a man, *any* man, and certainly not one with Jonah's easy smile, or his bottomless dark eyes, or his long-fingered, capable hands…

No, she told herself firmly. They were two ships sailing in opposite directions, alongside each other only long enough to signal hello.

She'd do well to remember that.

Still, she ran her tongue over her bottom lip, wondering what his might taste like.

"Hey," she said as he shoved the last box on top of the stack.

He turned, brushing the dust off his hands. "Kids gone?"

She nodded. "I locked the front door. Need any help back here?"

"I'm done. Are you taking Isaac and Gideon home?"

"My brother-in-law picked them up. He's taking them to the batting cages. All three of them are *obsessed* with baseball." She rolled her eyes.

"Not a sports fan?" He retrieved his pullover and yanked it over his head.

Damn.

"Nope, deep theater nerd. How about you?"

"I was a pretty competent third baseman once upon a time."

"Before you packed it all in to become a rabbi?"

"Something like that. Do you have plans tonight?"

"No," she said too quickly, taken aback, immediately wishing she'd been coyer.

"Why?" she asked, but it was too late—he was shrugging on his coat.

"Come on. I want to show you something."

"OH MY GOSH, Jonah," Ellie breathed, her eyes wide as she took in their surroundings. "How did I not know this was here?"

"Well, you don't really live around here anymore, do you?"

And I clearly don't come back often enough to visit, Ellie thought with a pang of regret, and then pushed her guilt aside. She was here now, and she intended to enjoy herself.

What had once been a dead, awkwardly shaped space between the side of the courthouse and the rear of a neighboring church was transformed into a festive outdoor dining experience. A semicircle of food trucks formed the border, each one brightly colored and open for business. Several picnic tables were in the center of the area, illuminated by strings of tiny lights crisscrossing between four poles, almost as if the tables sat beneath a low-hanging sky packed with glittering stars. Bundled-up customers moved from truck to truck, balancing cardboard containers in precarious mounds, climbing onto the wooden barrels scattered around the periphery that served as seats. The air sang with sounds of laughter and excitement, and it was all Ellie could do not to link her arm in Jonah's as if they were a couple—as if she had any claim to this glimpse of collective merriment.

"This way." Jonah grabbed her hand and tugged her toward one of the food trucks, his fingers entwined with hers as if this was no big deal, as if they were casual friends for whom hand-holding wasn't intimate or special.

As if the warmth of his skin didn't seem to set her whole body on fire, until she could hear nothing but the roar of the flames.

"Hey, Jonah! How've you been?" A man wearing a blue-and-white-striped apron greeted them as Jonah dropped her hand—the only reason she could begin to focus on where they'd arrived.

"Challah Back Boy," Ellie read from the sign, then looked down at the vendor with a groan. "That's terrible."

"It's hilarious," Jonah insisted. "Rob is the best kosher cook in town. His blueberry blintzes are so addictive, they should be illegal."

"No blintzes on the menu tonight, I'm afraid, but I've got latkes and sufganiyot. What can I get you two?"

Ellie didn't think twice. The salty, savory latkes smelled great, but the scent of the sweet, sinful fried dough of the sufganiyot made her mouth water.

"One strawberry sufganiyah, please."

"Make that two." Jonah handed over a few dollars, and

then they carried their powdered sugar-covered sufganiyot to the seating area on two little cardboard plates.

"We're just leaving." An older man stood up from one of the smaller picnic tables, a perfect fit for two, and gestured for them to sit. Across the table the woman Ellie assumed was his wife was already on her feet, brushing powdered sugar off her dark-blue jeans.

"Such a good-looking couple," the woman remarked with a smile. "How long have you been together?"

"We're not—" she and Jonah chimed in unison, then looked at each other and laughed.

"We just met last week," Ellie explained.

The man and his wife exchanged knowing glances.

"Well, enjoy your evening," he said, turning around and…

"Did he just wink at you?" Ellie asked once the couple were safely out of earshot.

"I hope not," Jonah muttered, then bit into his sufgani-yah.

Ellie did the same, closing her eyes as the light, fluffy doughnut-like pastry gave way to the gooey strawberry jam at the center. The dough practically melted in her mouth, and the jam was just the right combination of sweet and a little tart.

She opened her eyes to find Jonah watching her with a smile. "Good?"

"Perfect. Thanks for bringing me here."

"I owed you."

She frowned. "For what?"

"Taking one for the team with my dad today."

She squinted across the table at him, trying to understand what he meant. "About the Hebrew in the play?"

"And my penchant for big ideas I'm incapable of executing."

Ellie winced. "Right. Not sure where he got all that from. I think you're doing an awesome job, and the kids love you to pieces."

One side of Jonah's mouth briefly lifted in a humble smile. "Thanks. Unfortunately my dad has a tendency to focus on everything I do wrong, so it's nice to hear that occasionally I get things right."

"Sounds like you two have a tricky relationship."

Jonah nodded.

Ellie propped her chin on her hand, pushing her empty plate to one side to give him her full attention. "Want to tell me about it?"

He lifted a shoulder, easing back on the seat. "Typical father-son stuff, I guess. I spent my whole life trying to be exactly who he wanted, desperate to make him happy. Then I decided to make myself happy, and he's never gotten over the disappointment."

"Is this about your decision not to become a rabbi?"

He smiled, a little bitterly. "How'd you guess?"

"It follows that a rabbi would push his son to become

one, too."

"To be fair, he never pushed me. It was always my idea."

"So what happened?"

He took a deep breath, as if bracing himself. "I was in Israel for the first part of my seminary program. Have you been?"

She shook her head.

"It's an amazing place. Toward the end of the first semester I spent some time on a kibbutz. The community was so cool, unlike any I'd ever experienced. They try to live the original values of collectivism and sharing, but balanced that with progressive ideas about equality, education, opportunity. When I was there they were expanding their olive orchard, and I helped with the planting."

"That sounds awesome," she told him.

"I loved it. Loved working with my hands, going to bed with every muscle aching, and reading for fun and enrichment rather than obligation. It was the first time since high school that I wasn't spending hours a day buried in Torah study or trying to come up with bold, clever ideas for whatever essay I'd left until the last minute."

She smiled. "Story of my life, too."

He returned her grin with a sheepish one of his own. "I still thought of it as a well-deserved break. My dad had never been prouder than when he sent me on my way to Israel—the idea of quitting rabbinical school altogether hadn't entered my mind.

"Then," he said, pausing to pop a final piece of sufgani-yah in his mouth, "came Hanukkah."

She tilted her head, intrigued. "Not traditionally a time of self-reflection in the Jewish calendar."

"Not at all. A minor winter holiday marking a military victory as recorded in the Talmud. But I've learned that enlightenment has a funny way of creeping up on people, and on Hanukkah it caught me completely off guard."

She straightened, nodding for him to go on.

"A few people in the community decided to build a big menorah that everyone could light together on the eighth night. It was mostly for the kids, and one of the guys was a welder, so he pieced it out of scrap metal. Not a big deal—just a fun addition to the existing celebration."

Jonah stuck his thumb in his mouth and sucked off the last of the powdered sugar. Ellie watched, mesmerized. The way his cheeks pulled in, throwing his cheekbones into angular relief, those soft-looking lips curling around his thumb… Desire pounded so loudly in her ears it took her a second to realize he'd continued speaking.

Ellie swallowed hard, forcing herself back to the present.

These ridiculous flights of fancy need to stop, she told herself harshly. *You're leaving. He's staying. The end.*

"We had a great night. Good weather, lots of food, kids running around, everyone relaxed and celebrating. Someone had planted torches around the perimeter, and someone else thought it might be a good idea to take one with him when he walked back to his house. Ten minutes later we could see the flame from the orchard rising over the hill."

She gasped, pressing her hand over her mouth. "Oh no. What did you do?"

"The kibbutz had their own version of a volunteer fire department. I did a few hours of training with them when I first arrived, so they pulled me along as they ran to the orchard. The fire was raging, moving fast, threatening everything we'd all worked so hard for."

Jonah's eyes glittered, his gaze focused somewhere over her shoulder, undoubtedly seeing six thousand miles into the past, wading through memories of an experience she could only imagine.

She thought of the fire engulfing her apartment, the sudden, terrifying heat, the unstoppable speed with which it grew from an annoying mistake to a life-threatening catastrophe. She'd fled the apartment like death was at her heels—and perhaps it had been.

What sort of man not only chose not to turn away when danger beckoned, but ran straight toward it?

And how could anyone—let alone his own father—not appreciate how remarkable that made him?

Jonah inhaled, and when he met her eyes, she saw herself reflected clearly in their brown depths.

"It was hard, and scary—the scariest thing I've ever done. But we got the fire out and kept the damage to the orchard to a minimum. Afterward, when everything was cleaned up,

I walked back to where I was staying, through the central square. The menorah was still burning. Everyone else had gone home and I sat there, looking at the flames, thinking about what I'd just been part of—what I wanted to do with the rest of my life. The next morning I phoned the registrar's office and withdrew from seminary."

"Wow," Ellie murmured. "What was it that pushed you, in the end? The desire to be a firefighter? Or the realization that you didn't want to be a rabbi?"

"Neither—and both," he said, and they both smiled, a welcome respite from the weighty conversation. "I was definitely confident that I wouldn't be happy as a rabbi. I'd gone completely cold on the academic side, and while I sort of liked the idea of leading a congregation, it felt too narrow and self-selecting. Serving people who've already made the choice to participate in a temple community is absolutely important, but it didn't inspire me. I wanted to have big impact, even if only for a few minutes in the life of someone I'd never see again. That's why I ended up training as a firefighter-EMT, then a paramedic. The fire department was hiring when I moved down here, but once I get my paramedic license here in Missouri, I'll probably move over to do that full-time."

"That's so impressive, Jonah," she told him earnestly. "I can't see what part of all this your dad could possibly disapprove of. You save lives."

His expression darkened, and he dropped his gaze to his

linked hands resting on the table. "The career I chose is irrelevant. His complaint is that I quit."

"But there's no point in being ordained if you had no intention of remaining in the profession."

"He would disagree." Jonah smiled faintly. "Look, my father's not a bad guy—he's a terrific guy, in fact. A gifted rabbi and a great dad. If I'd always wanted to be something else, he would've supported it. My sister is in a grad program for archival studies, and he thinks it's a wonderful path. His problem is the pivot. That I pivoted away from his exact calling—and his father's calling, and his great-uncle's calling—certainly didn't help, but mostly he now thinks of me as a quitter. He hates that. This time of year the emotions around it are magnified by the holiday, since that's when I made the decision."

"Well, I could learn a thing or two about quitting," she said matter-of-factly. "I admire your decisiveness, and that you saw so clearly what you wanted—and what you didn't. For years I shoved what I really wanted to the side, promising myself I'd work on it tomorrow, or next week, or next year. Now I'm finally ready to make the move, but I wish I'd done it a long time ago."

"You mean acting in general, or going out to Los Angeles to do it?"

"Los Angeles. I worked in theater after college, just local stuff, a few projects for some of the schools, but I never focused on my own career, my own acting."

"Sounds like you spent some time on it, though. Did you enjoy it?"

"I did. My financial situation was unpredictable and mostly terrible, but I had so much fun, especially working in the schools, running workshops for kids, or assisting with their productions. I even got my teaching certificate, but something always came up that made me think I could still be an actress in my own right. An audition for a movie, or a part in a commercial—a little glimpse that my dream career might become reality."

He nodded, his forehead creased in thought. She adored how he took her seriously. So many other people made her feel like her dream was a frivolous fantasy—colleagues at work, not-boyfriend Jeff, even her sister sometimes. But Jonah seemed to weigh her words with as much sincerity as any other major decision, and she was grateful.

"Have you picked a date to give notice to the bank?"

"Not exactly. I had a number in mind, a total in my savings account, and I told myself I'd leave as soon as I hit it. I was nearly there, but I'll have to see how much the damage from the fire sets it back."

"So one extra paycheck? Two? Or are we talking six months?"

"Oh, nothing like that. Two, maybe three paychecks and I'll be there."

"Then why not quit now?"

For a second she simply stared at him, unable to process

his suggestion. "What?"

"You're talking about, what, a thousand dollars at most? You'll probably make it up when you sell your stuff to move out west. It's not a make-or-break figure, and it's the end of the year anyway. If you quit now, you could be popping champagne on New Year's Eve in sunny California."

"I could, I just—there are a couple of projects at work, and my apartment—"

"Your apartment is a smoke-damaged mess," Jonah reminded her, not unkindly. "And you hate your job, unless that's changed in the last day or two."

She shook her head. "No, I still hate it."

He smiled, broad and assured, and reached across the table to put his hand over hers. The evening air had gotten cold, and his palm was warm and firm, a reassuring weight.

She wondered what it would feel like to have his arms around her, steady and strong.

"Go. You have no reason to wait."

I have you.

The thought careened out of the darkness of her mind like a bat from under a bridge, so startling she jerked her hand out from under his.

She smiled apologetically but he withdrew his hand, his posture stiffening, like he thought she'd rebuffed him.

"Sorry, I didn't mean to…" Yes, she did. There could be nothing between them. Might as well rip off the bandage and let the wound start to heal.

"Maybe you're right. I've already moved a bunch of stuff out of my apartment—shifting it all back in for a month or six weeks would be a waste of time. Like you say, I've waited a long time, and not much is going to change. Maybe I should just take the plunge."

"As long as you wait until after the Hanukkah play."

"Of course."

She tried to look as grateful as she felt, but he stood up from the table and gathered their empty plates, carefully avoiding eye contact.

Fair enough, she told herself, trying to ignore a tugging sense of dejection. Anyway, he was right. Whatever the financial dent from the apartment fire, it wasn't fatal. She was due an end-of-year bonus that might make it a non-issue, and her most complicated projects at work had deadlines before the office closed for Christmas. She could make a clean break, tell everyone goodbye at the holiday party, and hang next year's calendar on a wall in Los Angeles.

She'd waited long enough. Nothing held her back. Her dream was in touching distance.

So why did she feel like she stood on the edge of a cliff, staring at the long drop, praying someone would grab her and pull her back to safety?

"I'll walk you to your car," Jonah said, reminding her that for now, at least, she stood on solid ground.

"Thank you. And thank you for bringing me here. Most of all, thanks for the advice. I needed it."

He ducked his head as if to say she was welcome, and then momentarily touched her elbow to guide her out of the brightly lit semicircle. They left behind the cheery clamor and mouthwatering scents, heading into the freezing darkness, the sidewalk barely illuminated in dim yellow by a humming, rickety streetlamp.

She glanced over her shoulder for one last look at the strings of lights overhanging the tables.

Each bulb shone white and clear, tiny filaments adding up to canopy of would-be stars.

Chapter Eight

H E WAITED FOR her like a ghost with a broken heart, watching from the shadows, restless, anxious, ignorant of time and so doomed never to realize how much of it had passed, or that all hope was long lost. The bedroom was dark, a book he pretended he planned to read closed on his lap. The white candles stood neatly in the brass menorah on the windowsill, four plus the shamash, ready to be lit.

Jonah didn't look at the time—he didn't want to know. He thought it might humiliate him to realize how long he'd been sitting here, unmoving beside the drafty window, hoping she would appear.

But why would she? He'd clearly misread the signals— wrongly assumed there were any signals being sent. He told himself he just wanted to show her the kosher food truck, treat her to something tasty to say thank-you for the way she handled his dad's criticism at the rehearsal. He should never have given in to his instinct to touch her, that hard-swallowing urge to physically connect, to feel her hand against his.

He cringed, closing his eyes and pinching the bridge of

his nose as he recalled the way she'd yanked her hand out from beneath his. What was he thinking? He wasn't, not at all.

Maybe his dad was right. Maybe he was all lofty ideas floating way above his head, with no grounding in reality.

Jonah looked around the room, stripped to plasterboard and unvarnished floorboards, and smirked. He loved this old house, but right now he couldn't think of a better example to prove his dad's point. He'd rushed into the purchase, following his heart, ignoring his head's protests that it was an awfully big renovation project for one man on a shoestring budget.

He didn't regret it for a second, especially when the morning sunlight slanted through the kitchen, or he caught a glimpse of the sunset from a bedroom bathed in orange glow.

But he probably should've at least gotten a few quotes for repairs before he signed on the dotted line.

With a sigh of resignation Jonah shifted in the chair—an uncomfortable, cushion-less refugee from an incomplete dining set he'd picked up at a thrift store. He'd migrated it to his bedroom purely for storage purposes—he regularly dragged it from one end to the other so it doubled as a nightstand and a coat hook—and its uselessness as an actual seat had become apparent.

He stood, stretching his arms over his head. Time to get real. She wasn't coming.

Jonah picked up the book that had slid off his knee and tossed it onto the chair. He took a couple steps to the bed and leaned across it to grab his phone when he saw a flash of movement in his peripheral vision.

Ellie stood in her window, smiling tentatively as she raised her hand in greeting.

Elation surged through him with an adrenaline chaser, and he had to carefully pace his steps back to his chair so it didn't look like he was sprinting across the room.

He brushed the book back onto the floor and resumed his seat, trying not to grin like a fool, cautioning himself not to get excited. This was the fourth night they'd done this, after all. It didn't signify anything beyond a friendly connection.

With a small nod of acknowledgment they began to light their candles in unison. Jonah muttered the blessing under his breath, feeling oddly self-conscious despite being alone in his room. Their dynamic had changed, at least on his end. He knew it was foolish, but he'd begun to care about how Ellie thought of him. He wanted her to like him—or more than like him.

He shook his head in exasperation as his hand moved the shamash from one wick to the next, anointing each with a bright orange blaze. In the long run, sure, he wanted a relationship, a solid marriage, eventually a family. He'd dated on and off, but romance had always taken a back seat to the bigger issues in front of him—school, ordination, a new career, uprooting to St. Louis and starting over yet again. Between teaching at Temple Sinai, fixing up his money-pit house, and attempting to thaw his icy relationship with his dad, he honestly hadn't given his love life any thought for months.

Until now.

Of course it would be someone like Ellie—clever, capable, with one foot out the door on her way to a brand-new life on the other side of the country. He couldn't follow her—he wouldn't follow anyone or anything anywhere until he'd shown his dad he could commit, and put them back on an even keel. He wasn't the short-term type, either, ironic though that seemed given his dad's opinions. Just wasn't in his nature. He'd never been able to fake interest to get what he wanted, because he only ever wanted genuine connection.

Exactly like what he felt was building with Ellie.

He replaced the shamash with a muted sigh, reminding himself that whatever he felt probably wasn't reciprocated. Hopefully that would make it easier to ignore.

At any rate, they were halfway to the play. This time next week they'd be strangers again, barely exchanging a neighborly wave if they happened to pass on the sidewalk.

He raised his hand to say goodbye, but Ellie held up her palms as if to tell him to stop. She shoved her menorah aside, the candles wobbling dangerously as she reached around it to unlatch the window and push it open.

"Hey," she called, and he nodded toward her menorah,

taking a little longer to urge his rickety window frame up high enough to let in a blast of freezing air.

"Careful," he warned, and she righted one of the candles just as it looked ready to fall right out.

"Thanks. You're a great firefighter, but I'd rather not require your services twice in one week."

"I don't take it personally. What's up?"

"You were right. I'm going to do it. I need to wait a couple days to qualify for my end-of-year bonus, then I'm quitting my job. I already looked at flights and sent a couple of emails to rental agencies in LA. You gave me the push I needed, Jonah. Thank you."

He smiled. He was happy for her, and he was happy she was happy. That thick knot of selfish disappointment clenching in the pit of his stomach could go to hell.

"That's great, Ellie. I'm glad I was able to help."

"You did more than help. You showed me there's nothing wrong with chasing what you want. I know your dad doesn't think so, but for what it's worth, I have nothing but admiration for you. And I wanted to say… If things were different… If I weren't…"

She trailed off, biting her lower lip. He waited, giving her the space to say whatever she needed, though as the seconds ticked past her expression grew more and more conflicted. It was dark, and the glow from the candles could be misleading, but…was she blushing?

"Oh," she exclaimed, extending her hand through the

window. "It's snowing!"

Jonah blinked, shifting his focus from her to the thickly cloudy sky above them. Sure enough, a few delicate white flakes drifted down, swirling slightly as they caught on the light breeze.

He dropped his gaze again to find Ellie watching him, her lips shaped by a wistful, almost regretful smile.

He didn't understand what it meant, wanted to know what she'd been about to say with sudden, intense urgency, but it was too late. He heard Isaac and Gideon running down the front steps, their excited voices audible from the side of the house. Ellie's expression settled into careful, friendly neutrality as she took a step back from the window.

"I'd better go help make sure my nephews don't get hypothermia. See you tomorrow?"

He nodded—he couldn't do anything else. "See you tomorrow."

She slammed the window shut and left, a blurry shape vanishing into the darkness. He remained, dumbfounded, staring at the still-burning candles on her menorah as if they might give him a clue about what just happened.

He shook his head to clear it and rose from his chair. Whatever he thought he'd seen, he probably hadn't. And if he had—if by some rare chance he'd gotten a glimpse of rueful longing that exactly matched his own—what did it matter? She'd already looked at flights, was days away from leaving her job.

All thanks to his helpful advice, he thought, finding a wry smile.

"That's that," he announced to himself, easing the old wooden-framed window back down. He'd focus on being happy for Ellie, wishing her well on her new path, and watching for her name in lights.

Still, something dangerous flared in his chest, as bright and hot as the candles on the windowsill. Something treacherous, unwelcome, and wildly misplaced.

Hope.

Chapter Nine

ELLIE MEANDERED DOWN the sidewalk, her boots leaving gray prints in the slush. She had twenty minutes to kill before the bakery opened—if she'd known it didn't open until ten she wouldn't have volunteered to make a coffee-and-doughnut run—so she didn't hurry as she made her way down Main Street, lingering in front of whichever shop windows caught her interest.

Most of them were closed this Sunday morning, but she was impressed nonetheless. She'd spent so little time in Orchard Hill since her mom died, she hadn't realized how much the neighborhood had changed. A sleek wine bar had taken the place of the grimy pub that reeked of cigarettes from halfway down the block. The outdated haircutters' had become a high-end salon and spa. Even the jewelers' shop, a family business dating back fifty years at least, had undergone a facelift now that one of the daughters was at the helm. Ellie gazed wistfully at the crisp, stylish diamond rings in the case. Sure, her career was on the brink of takeoff—but what woman didn't fantasize about having a sparkler on her finger, and the man who would put it there?

She reached the end of the block and turned, taking in the full length of Main Street. The turn-of-the-century facades were decorated in wreaths and garlands for the holidays, the hundred-year-old streetlamps capped by the still-pristine snowfall from last night. The one-way road ended in a dead end dominated by the looming figure of the old movie theater, complete with its original vertical marquee, which had been converted into Orchard Hill's most glamorous restaurant and event space.

Had her little suburb always seemed this sweet and welcoming, or was she just being nostalgic now she so clearly had an exit plan?

She used to love coming back for the weekend, waking up in her childhood bedroom, the peace and quiet a relaxing respite from her cramped downtown apartment and hectic career. Come to think of it, she'd probably worked more hours back then, constantly juggling her existing teaching commitments with auditioning, performing, and pitching for more work in the school system.

Funny to think how busy she'd been. She'd worked harder for far less money, yet she never felt drained like she did now. Exactly the opposite, in fact. Yes, the obligations on her time were myriad and underpaid, but everything she did energized her and made her hungry for more. She loved theater—she always had. The immersion in the story, the camaraderie among the cast and crew, the unselfconscious space to be her most creative self… Each day, each hour was ripe with possibility, the pages in the calendar flying by as she stuffed her life with as much of her passion for theater as she could grab.

Now the weeks dragged. Her bank account bulged but she met the first of each month with dread, totally devoid of enthusiasm for the work that lay ahead.

Still, she'd avoided coming here, buried herself forehead-deep in the daily misery rather than risk the ghosts that haunted her hometown. She didn't want to sip coffee at the same table where she sat with her mom after buying a prom dress. Couldn't walk past the post office without remembering hours she'd spent fidgeting at the counter while her mom gossiped with her favorite teller. She heard her mom call from around every corner, saw her in every turned back walking through a chiming door, felt her in every footstep, every inch she moved through this tranquil, innocuous suburb.

Ellie knew she was being unfair. Orchard Hill hadn't killed her mother, or her father—Orchard Hill gave her family more than it ever took.

Orchard Hill had provided an idyllic backdrop for her childhood, even in the wake of her father's death. The school system was good, the area was safe, the suburb was within easy reach of all the benefits of St. Louis, yet the community was humble and not ostentatious. Today it was still a haven for young families like her sister's, and the density and lack of room for new development—and the fact that most residents were so content, they stayed put until they died—meant most new buyers had some extensive renovations on their hands. Maybe she was biased, but she liked the way Orchard Hill valued historical preservation as one by one the old homes were refreshed and renewed, yet honored, restored to their former glory rather than bulldozed and rebuilt. She loved that this community was still accessible to hard-working people ready to invest more elbow grease than money.

Like Jonah.

The thought of him spurred her into motion, as if she could power-walk away from the uncomfortable emotions that kept her up way too late last night.

Hollow-stomached yearning. Thrumming, pulse-quickening desire. And fear—fear that he didn't want her, that one day he would want someone else, that if left unacknowledged much longer this blossoming something between them would wither and crumble and vanish forever, never to be replicated with anyone else.

She told herself it was a simply a reaction to upcoming change, a normal psychological response in the form of a desire to hold on to something while so much else slid away.

A theory worth about as much as she'd paid for it, which was precisely nothing.

Light glinted on glass, snagging in her peripheral vision, and she stopped, then walked five steps in reverse. That flicker had been the door of Second Chance swinging shut, meaning the shop was open for business this Sunday morning.

She checked her phone. Still ten minutes before she could go to the bakery. Plenty of time to pick up some additional props—by which she absolutely meant browse for gorgeous trinkets for her new apartment, and then take an old piece of clutter off Noa's hands to make herself feel better.

Silver bells tinkled as Ellie pushed open the door. She paused, inhaling a lungful of the sumptuous, wintry scent pervading the interior—pine, peppermint, and a touch of vanilla. Music played gently in the background, and the warm lighting immediately made her feel like she'd stepped out of slushy Missouri and into a holiday-season fairy tale.

"Oh my gosh, this store is a—hi, Mrs. Futter."

Ellie smiled sheepishly at her mom's old friend and Temple Sinai stalwart, pulling back the arms she'd flung open in dramatic expression.

"Eliana," Mrs. Futter greeted her kindly, sliding a picture frame across the counter for Noa to ring up. "I didn't know you were back in town. Is this a flying visit or are you here for a while?"

"I'm staying with my sister while my apartment is…being renovated. And I'm helping out with the Hanukkah play this year. How's Richie?" she asked, referencing the son Mrs. Futter had spent years trying to set up with her.

"Oh, he's wonderful. Engaged! The wedding's in June.

She's an absolute treasure—a lawyer, and she volunteers at an animal shelter twice a month. Richie's orthodontics practice is so busy, he's looking at hiring two more assistants. We couldn't be prouder. And you? Are you still acting?"

"Yes. In fact, I'm moving to Los Angeles in a couple of weeks."

"That's terrific." Mrs. Futter smiled benevolently, passing her credit card to Noa. "You were always so talented. Your mom would be proud."

"Thank you," Ellie said softly as Mrs. Futter signed the receipt, trying hard to believe this woman she'd known most of her life. Mrs. Futter was probably right—her mom was proud of pretty much anything she did, from kindergarten scrawls to the Latin honors on her bachelor's degree. And she'd always regretted that Ellie's flirtation with child stardom hadn't developed into anything more. Ellie didn't blame her in the least—funding acting lessons or a summer at an East Coast theater camp couldn't be a priority for a newly widowed mom of two—but she'd always sensed a disproportionate personal investment on her mom's part, like Ellie's contentment with and even enthusiasm for local theater was proof that some distant, faded, long-ago dream of Hollywood wasn't totally dead.

So why did she have an increasingly nagging feeling that moving to LA wouldn't have made her mom happy at all?

"Lovely to run into you, Eliana. Remember us back here in Orchard Hill when you're a Hollywood starlet!"

"I will," Ellie promised, waving goodbye as Mrs. Futter breezed out the door.

"Nice to see you again." Noa smiled, ducking into an employee area hidden by a partial wall.

Ellie picked up a beautifully embroidered baby dress. "It won't be the last time. I'm obsessed with this store. Especially since you're open on a Sunday morning."

"Well, there is a big Jewish community in Orchard Hill. And this time of year, with gift-giving season in full swing, I'll open whenever I can manage it."

"Is it just you here? Or do you have other people who help out?"

"I have two assistants—both moms who take shifts during school hours. Then I take over for the afternoons, evenings, and weekends. It's working well so far. Tea?"

"Oh, don't go to any trouble," Ellie protested, but Noa was already returning with two steaming mugs in her hands.

"Cranberry Cinnamon Wonderland," Noa announced as Ellie took one of the mugs. "I met a lady who hand-blends her own teas from her home in Hi-Pointe. I'm thinking of stocking them here—you can be my beta tester. Yummy? Likely to appeal to the good citizens of Orchard Hill?"

Ellie took a sip, frowning as she let the flavors roll around her mouth, then burst into a grin. "Delicious."

"Excellent!" Noa exclaimed, and then propped one hip against the counter. "So, LA, huh? I lived out there for a while."

"Really?"

"I lived pretty much everywhere, or so it felt. My mom's an artist—she likes to move around. LA was all right. Expensive. We had a tiny apartment. My mom got some work as an extra. Once she even had her name in the credits, as Murder Victim. Big-time stuff." Noa smiled.

"Did you like it?"

She shrugged. "It was fine. The weather was good. I was in middle school—the kids were nice, mostly."

"You don't sound like you loved it."

"Honestly, no. But I don't like big cities—too impersonal, too rush-rush-rush. That's why I settled here in Orchard Hill. It's a low-ego place with great community spirit. But then, I'm not an aspiring actress, and you have to go where the work is, right?"

"Right," Ellie agreed, all too aware of how unconvinced she sounded.

"I'm sure you'll love it," Noa assured her. "And it'll be Orchard Hill's loss. Spoiler alert, but a bunch of parents have been in to buy gifts for you to say thanks for your work on the Hanukkah play. If it's even half as good as they say, it'll be next stop: Broadway."

Ellie laughed. "I'm not sure the Temple Sinai Hanukkah play could pack the house in New York, but I'm glad the kids are enjoying themselves."

Noa sipped her tea, then suddenly pointed at Ellie as if she'd just thought of something. Ellie waited for her to swallow, smiling bemusedly.

"I can't believe I didn't think of this," Noa said eventually, a little hoarse from gulping the hot liquid. "Do you know Dana Gregson?"

Ellie squinted, searching for the name. "Does she teach at Francis Murdoch Elementary? I think my sister mentioned her."

"She's the principal. She was in the other day, buying a gift for their drama teacher—she's going on maternity leave. She mentioned they're having interviews tomorrow and asked if I knew anyone who might be interested. I guess they're really struggling to find people, since it's only a part-time contract, and a temporary one at that. I don't know when you're leaving for Los Angeles but maybe—"

"Before the end of the year," Ellie told her squarely, not even daring to be tempted by the prospect of returning to the classroom—at her nephews' school, no less.

Years ago it would've been a golden opportunity. Now that she was finally heading in a different direction, no way was she turning back.

Noa's face flashed with disappointment she then quickly tucked behind an encouraging smile. "Oh. Well, good for you."

"Thanks. And thanks for the tea. I need to get going—the bakery should be open now." Ellie forced brightness into her tone as she checked the time and put down her mug. Her eagerness to browse had deflated like a leaky balloon.

"Of course. Thanks for stopping in."

Ellie raised her palm in farewell and had her hand on the door when Noa called her name from behind the counter.

"Do you want Dana's number, just in case? Worst-case scenario, you spend forty-five minutes talking about a job you won't take. Best-case scenario, you have a backup plan. You never know, by this time tomorrow all of Hollywood could be buried in a mudslide."

Ellie hesitated. Would she undermine herself by agreeing? Would it be an admission that she might *not* be on her way to LA, that in a month's time she might be exactly where she'd been for the last two years? Acknowledging the possibility this might all be yet another false start felt dangerous, like she was dooming herself to fail before she'd even tried.

On the other hand, Noa had a point. It sounded like a good job—a great job, if she was honest with herself. Exactly the kind of job she would've leaped at before her mom got sick. Would it be the worst thing in the world to go along and hear them out? It never hurt to network.

Ellie dropped her hand from the door and stepped back into the shop. "Actually, yes. I'd love Dana's number. Thanks for the suggestion. And thanks for thinking of me for this job."

Noa grinned as she picked up her phone. "It's all yours."

Chapter Ten

JONAH SHOVED THE last box on top of the pile, then stood back and brushed off his hands. Temple Sinai's immaculately tidy, concrete-floored storage room was several degrees cooler than the rest of the building, but every time he was in here he was stacking chairs or hoisting boxes so he barely felt the cold. Today was no different, as he spent a good ten minutes after each rehearsal completely packing up the props and costumes they'd used for the Hanukkah play and stowing everything out of the way. Annoying and tedious— it'd be much easier if they could simply throw the stuff into the boxes and leave them at the back of the classroom—but he didn't want an argument with his dad over mess from the Hanukkah play.

Not that they'd spoken to each other much these last few days—or at all, come to think of it. Friday-night service had been as awkward as usual, with Jonah diligently attending and participating, while his father's eyes skipped over him as he addressed the congregation. At Oneg Shabbat he hovered halfway to the exit, chatting distractedly with the parents of some of his students, desperate to get home and use some of his limited free time to address the long list of urgent repairs in his house, but too conscious of his father's watchful attention.

He could imagine his dad ranting to his mom in the car on the way home. *Jonah didn't even stay to help clean up after Oneg Shabbat—is it any wonder he gave up on ordination? All those years of dedication and study, and he throws it away after one puny fire in Israel. Maybe it's a blessing in disguise—he clearly wasn't cut out to be a rabbi in the first place.*

So this week, as he did every week, he'd stayed until the bitter end. He cleaned and carried and organized. He even helped ninety-three-year-old Mrs. Finkelstein out to her car, which she'd inexplicably parked in the farthest possible space from the door—although the flirty way she stroked his arm and the saucy wink she threw him as he waved her off may have had something to do with it.

His reward was a curt nod from his father, a smile from his mother, and going to bed in a house that was still a complete wreck.

Jonah sighed, surveying the nice, neat pile of boxes his father probably never noticed. Sometimes he wondered if he and his dad would ever get back to the way they were—and in the same breath knew he wouldn't stop trying until they did.

He turned to leave—and nearly had a heart attack.

"Isaac, you can't sneak up on people like that," he told the boy in the doorway. "You scared me half to death."

"Sorry," the five-year-old said in a small voice, remaining where he stood.

"What're you doing here? Did I forget a box in the sanctuary?"

Isaac stared at him.

Jonah softened his tone. "Did something happen? You can tell me—you won't get into trouble."

The little boy's lower lip stuck out.

"All right, let's get out of this room, it's freezing. Stand over here and we'll talk about it." He ushered Isaac into the hallway, switched off the lights, and shut the storage-room door. Then he dropped to Isaac's level, one knee on the floor, and asked, "What's up?"

Isaac burst into tears.

It took about five minutes of gentle back-patting, arm-squeezing, and murmured assurances that everything would be fine before Isaac managed to say anything coherent. By the time he did Jonah's foot was asleep and his knee ached, but he kept his gaze on Isaac's, trying to show the boy that he was listening and he took him seriously.

"I don't want to be a Temple Restorer," Isaac muttered, the words distorted and stuck together as he worked to pull himself together.

"Why not? You don't have to speak on stage if it's making you nervous; we can change that part," Jonah offered, remembering his father's criticism. Maybe he *was* putting too much pressure on these kids.

Isaac shook his head. "It's not that, it's…it's…"

"It's what?"

Isaac took a few hitching breaths, then let out a stream of words with so little space in between each one it took Jonah a second to decipher the sentence. "I told a kid at school I was a Temple Restorer and he said what's that and I said it's a cleaner who cleans up the temple and he laughed at me and he said that's a dumb job and I said no it's not and he said yes it is and I said I even talk in the play and he said cleaning is stupid and he kicked sand at me and I ignored him and walked away like my mom says but also I don't want to be a Temple Restorer anymore I want to be a Maccabee and have a sword."

Isaac sucked in some air, and then his face crumpled as a fresh wave of tears overtook him.

After another minute or two of calming Isaac down— Jonah took the opportunity to shift from one knee to the other—the boy's sobs had reduced to hiccups. He gazed at Jonah so pleadingly, he had to work hard to suppress an affectionate smile.

"I think you know what I'm going to say. Have a guess."

"I can't be a Maccabee and I have to stay as a Temple Restorer. But I don't *want* to," Isaac protested sulkily.

"And why do you think I want you to be a Temple Restorer?"

"Because all the big kids are being the Maccabees."

Jonah shook his head. "Because it's one of the most important roles, and the kid who told you otherwise has no idea what he's talking about."

"But it's just cleaning," Isaac said disdainfully. "Picking up things off the floor and sweeping. I want a sword, not a broom."

Jonah had to smile at Isaac's inadvertently poetic encapsulation of the history of the human ego. "Almost everyone does. But what sort of world would we live in if everyone was a fighter and no one was a fixer?"

He shrugged, his mouth an upside-down U.

"Maybe cleaning the temple doesn't seem glamorous or brave, but it's essential. The Temple Restorers are some of the most important people in the story. The miracle didn't occur on the battlefield—it was in the temple, a tiny amount of oil burning for eight nights, lighting the way for the restorers and the rededication."

Isaac looked unconvinced. Jonah studied him for a moment, trying to figure out how to translate big, grown-up ideas into the language of a five-year-old.

"Remember we talked about tikkun olam in class? What does it mean?"

"Improving the world for everyone," Isaac repeated dutifully.

"We talked about some examples, too. Were they all huge things, like being elected president or giving away everything you own to someone else?"

Isaac shook his head. "Tikkun olam can be small, like

helping Mom carry the groceries, or picking up litter."

"Or cleaning."

The little boy bit his lip, considering this, and then he nodded.

"Everyone has their part to play in making the world a better place. Sometimes the smallest acts can be the most important."

"I guess so," Isaac said thoughtfully, and then brightened. "Because there wouldn't even have been a miracle if no one went into the temple to fix it, right? And found the oil? And then no one could've gone inside because it would've been full of broken stuff and trash."

Jonah smiled at his youthful interpretation of the ancient story. "Exactly."

"Next time I'm at school I'm going to tell that boy he's wrong."

"I have a better idea. Why don't you give him another chance to be your friend? Maybe he didn't understand the story, or maybe he was just having a bad day. We all need a do-over sometimes."

Isaac wrinkled his nose. "What if I play with someone else and only be nice to him if he tries to play with me?"

"Deal."

"Thanks, Mr. Jonah." Isaac grinned, then turned on his heel and sprinted down the hall, already onto the next pressing issue in the world of a kindergartener.

Slowly Jonah straightened, his knees stiff and creaking as

he pushed up off the floor. He wasn't getting any younger, he thought, kneading his lower back. Past time to put down some roots, establish himself somewhere for the long-term. He had the house, he noted as he turned, now he just needed—

"Ellie. I didn't see you there."

"Because I was hiding around the corner. I didn't want to interrupt your conversation with Isaac." She stepped fully into the hallway. "You gave him good advice."

"Thanks. I wish I could take it, for my own sake."

She cocked her head to one side. "What do you mean?"

"Just this stuff with my dad. Working on the Hanukkah play has made me think about what it'll take to make him happy, and whether it's even possible. I should focus on my own tikkun olam and my impact on the world as I see it, and stop trying to look through his eyes and do what I think he wants."

"Even better advice."

"Too bad I can't seem to follow it."

"You will, one day. These things take time."

"I hope so, because something needs to change."

"It will," she told him confidently, and he tried his best to believe her.

She shifted from one foot to the other, crossing her arms. "I might be late to rehearsal tomorrow. I have a job interview."

"Like an audition? For something in LA?"

She shook her head. "Maternity cover for the drama teacher at Murdoch Elementary."

"The one here in Orchard Hill?"

Ellie nodded.

"I'm confused. I thought you were full steam ahead on moving to California?"

"I am. This is just a backup option, in case it all goes wrong. But it won't. I'm leaving for Los Angeles before this year is over," she insisted, but it was too late—a dangerous ember of hope glowed in the center of his chest, stirring, brightening.

"Always good to have a plan B."

"Exactly. And that's all this is. I probably won't get the job, anyway."

He doubted that, but he kept his mouth shut. Selfishly he wanted her to stay, wanted her to feel as settled here as he did—maybe even to find room in her life for him, in one way or another.

But he was the one who encouraged her to be decisive and finally make the move to LA. Who was he to stand in the way of her dreams? Anyway, even if she stayed, she might not give him the time of day once the play finished. She might go straight back to whoever she'd been waiting for that night her romantic dinner turned into a towering inferno.

No, she won't, chimed a disloyal voice in the back of his mind. *You've seen the way she looks at you. If you made the first move, there's no way you'd be rejected.*

Tempting—but he didn't dare. Even if she was interested in being more than whatever they were—codirectors, sort-of friends, secret nighttime candle lighters—he wouldn't derail her plans. If she really wanted to leave, to pursue a path she'd waited so long to start down, he'd wish her well and wave goodbye.

And always wonder what might have been.

"Good luck with it," he said, forcing a smile. "Don't worry about the rehearsal. I'll get started without you."

"Thanks."

She hesitated, looking like she had something else to say, and then abruptly changed her mind. "I'd better get the boys home. See you later?"

He heard the question and knew exactly what she meant.

"Later," he promised.

Ellie smiled, lifting her hand in a brisk farewell. Then she turned and strode off down the hall, strawberry-blond hair bouncing against her back as she walked.

He watched her go, amazed that someone he'd known for less than a week had managed to squeeze herself into places in his heart that had been empty for so long, he'd practically forgotten they existed. They'd be vacant again soon—teaching job or not, she seemed bound and determined to turn her back on Orchard Hill for good.

He couldn't blame her. This town undoubtedly held a lot of difficult memories for her—her parents' passing, the loss and grief and their absence in her life.

But it had its good points, too. Her sister. Her nephews. Him.

He scoffed, stepping back into the storage room to double-check everything was put away. Even if she did decide to stay, if they did become more than friends, what did he have to offer her? A poorly paid career with irregular hours, a collapsing pit of a house...

...and his heart. All of it. Forever.

"Sentimental nonsense," he muttered harshly, shoving a box more firmly onto the shelf. Clearly the festive season had gone to his head. In a few days the play would be over, their menorahs packed away, the nights dark and cold.

Ellie would be gone, and he'd be back to piecing together the rest of his life.

He switched off the light in the storage room, standing for a moment in the pitch black. Then he made his way toward the sliver of light from the hallway, stepped outside, and slammed the door shut.

Chapter Eleven

"WOW. JUST WOW." Dana Gregson studied the stapled sheaf of papers in her hand, then looked back up at Ellie. "I wasn't expecting this level of creativity and professionalism in an applicant for a part-time contract. I'm going to be honest with you—I'm blown away."

Ellie's cheeks heated with a happy flush. "I've always been passionate about curriculum design and ways to engage students who don't seem like natural fits for theater studies. I know it's been a while since I've actively worked in education, but—"

Dana waved off her protest. "You're clearly up-to-date with progressions in the pedagogy."

"It's kind of a hobby," Ellie admitted.

"And you're prepared to relocate to Orchard Hill for a while? I see the address on your CV is in the Central West End. That's a tough commute."

It should've been an easy question. *Oh yes, I'm staying with my sister. She lives less than half a mile from Murdoch Elementary. You might know my nephews—Gideon is in second grade and Isaac just started kindergarten.*

Instead she balked. The words dried up in her mouth, and she stared at the principal, her tongue in knots.

Relocate to—*live* in—Orchard Hill? She couldn't. She wouldn't—not temporarily, not even for pretend so she could secure a job. She'd promised herself a long time ago that she was done with this place, and the thought of reneging had anxiety squeezing her lungs until each breath was a scratchy, rasping drag.

"Actually, I—the commute isn't—I'm not sure where—"

Too late—the brightly lit enthusiasm in Dana's expression dimmed.

"Let's not get ahead of ourselves. I enjoyed our meeting, and I appreciate you taking the time to come in. I'll confer with my team and get back to you shortly."

"Thank you for your consideration." Ellie leaped to her feet in unison with Dana. They shook hands and said their goodbyes, and Ellie held her breath until she was safely out of the principal's office. Then she let it out in one big sigh of relief.

She hated to admit it to herself, but she really wanted this job. It would be a perfect transition back into the classroom, paid enough to keep her afloat while she got back in the rhythm of local auditions, and could open the door to something full-time and permanent in the future. If it had come along three years ago, she would've bitten off her own hand to secure the offer.

But she was so close to starting over—on the verge of

putting almost two thousand miles between her and all the pain and grief that clung to every inch of this town.

Although that also meant she'd be two time zones away from Jonah.

She glanced at her phone—she couldn't dwell on all of that right now. They only had two rehearsals left before the performance, and she'd already missed most of this one.

She'd left work early under the guise of attending a doctor's appointment, trying to make it sound potentially serious in the hope that would limit her colleagues' inclinations to bother her. Unfortunately she underestimated them, and by the time she parked outside Temple Sinai she'd already fielded several calls. She sat in her car and frantically worked through some emails on her phone, trying to delegate or deflect enough to leave her free to concentrate on the rehearsal. Instead they prompted more responses and phone calls, and by the time she rushed up the walkway to the front door, the first parent had arrived to pick up their child.

"Jonah, I'm so sorry," she called, jogging down the aisle toward the raised platform where the kids were dutifully depositing their props and costumes into waiting boxes. She hurried to where Jonah stood and instinctively grabbed his wrist—then dropped it like it was on fire.

"Sorry," she repeated as he fixed her with a quizzical smile.

"It's fine. How did it go?"

"Good, I think. Let me help you get everything put

away."

Parents began to arrive in greater numbers, and Ellie spent the next twenty minutes fielding questions from kids, promising to fix costumes or blocking or lines, and trying not to feel too awkward when their moms and dads doled out compliments. Eventually Dan came to pick up Gideon and Isaac, and after a wave and the assurance she'd be home for dinner, she and Jonah were alone.

"I can't believe I missed the whole rehearsal. Thank you so much for stepping up—I owe you," she told him.

"No, you don't." He dropped into the first-row pew and stretched his long legs out in front of him, then patted the space at his side. "Sit. Tell me how it went."

She sat beside him, excitement heating her cheeks anew as she processed her interview. "It was great. The principal and I had a good, easy rapport, and I think she was impressed by my ideas. The role itself is right up my alley, working one day a week with each grade level in the school. Obviously it's temporary, just covering next semester while the normal drama teacher is on leave, but she said they have budget for an additional part-timer in the fall. It could easily lead to something permanent."

"You sound like you're genuinely considering it."

"I do, don't I," Ellie replied softly, her enthusiasm faltering. She wrung her hands in her lap, her emotions tangling into a tight, muddled knot.

He elbowed her gently. "Talk to me."

She turned toward him suddenly, seeing him as if for the first time. His dark eyes held hers calmly, his expression patient and attentive. For years she'd spent all day, every day answering questions, addressing other people's needs. She couldn't remember when last anyone had looked at her like that—with openness, honesty, and true interest.

Ellie took a deep breath, but it did nothing to steady her fluttering heart.

"I'm a mess," she told him, and immediately felt some of the tension melt from her shoulders. "A few years ago I would've thrown myself at this job. It's exactly what I wanted back then—the chance to work with kids, to spend all my time living and breathing theater, with a little financial stability to boot. On paper the job itself still looks great, but everything else around it has changed so much. My mom is gone. No more medical bills, no more weekend stays in her house, no more spotting her smile from the front row on opening night, no more calls just to say—"

Ellie broke off, covering her mouth with her hand as the tears came fast and hot. She squeezed her eyes shut, her breaths hitching, but it was too late. She couldn't stop the sobs that shook her entire body.

"I'm sorry, Jonah, this is not—"

He wrapped his arms around her and pulled her against his chest, cutting off her apology with a quiet shush. She stiffened, determined not to let him see her this way—but she was no match for the warm weight of his arms or the reassuring strength of his grip.

Ellie sagged against him, her whole body going limp. His chin brushed the top of her head, and she pressed her forehead into the space just below his throat, his cotton crewneck shirt soft against her cheek. She tightened her own arms around the breadth of his ribs and cried, clinging to Jonah like a tree branch extended over the rushing stream of her emotions. Grief, pain, loneliness, regret, confusion, and profound despair all fought to pull her under, but Jonah's grasp was firm, and she knew she was safe as long as he held her tightly.

She didn't know how long it took for the swirling current to recede, but eventually it did—and embarrassment seeped into its place. She eased back, sniffing hard, too mortified to meet Jonah's eyes as she wiped her cheeks.

"Sorry. This is a hard time of year."

"Hey." With a finger under her chin he tilted her face up, forcing her to look him in the eyes. "Stop apologizing."

She managed a sheepish smile. "I'll try."

"It sounds to me like this is about more than a part-time teaching job. This is a decision about the rest of your life—whether you stay in Orchard Hill and rebuild what you used to have, or you move to Los Angeles and start over."

"Gee, no pressure when you put it like that," she joked.

Ellie studied her hands clasped in her lap. Last night she'd painted her nails a rich purple shade called SoCal Sunset. She'd bought the bottle months ago but never used it, stupidly worried she might jinx something. Her thumbnail was already chipped; she used it to twist the sapphire ring she wore on her right hand, a family heirloom passed down from her grandmother to her mother to her.

She looked up at Jonah. "What do you think I should do?"

He didn't answer—he didn't have to. She saw the subtle change in his expression, the shift from the sensible, King Solomon wisdom he wore so naturally to something hungrier, more selfish.

His hand drifted up to her neck, his palm warm and dry against her skin. His thumb traced the line of her jaw, leaving what felt like a streak of fire in its wake. The sensation grew and pulsed and intensified until her whole body burned with need.

She pressed her hand over his and watched his eyes darken with desire, two pools of molten tar, ready to be ignited. He tilted his head, silently asking her permission. In answer she inched closer, smiled, and closed her eyes.

She sensed him lean in, filled her lungs with his crisp scent, her heart beating so hard she could feel its thudding in the pit of her stomach. She hadn't expected this—didn't dare imagine it might even be a possibility—but now that the moment was here, she wanted it more than anything. Never mind the future and what this could or shouldn't mean. Right now she needed Jonah to kiss her. Nothing else mattered.

She turned her face up, parting her lips ever so slightly, holding her breath as she anticipated the sudden pressure of his mouth, the welcome intrusion of his tongue. He was close enough for her to feel the heat of his body, hear the soft rasp of air in his throat. She could practically taste his desire, thick and throbbing. He wanted this as much as she did.

But he hesitated.

She opened her eyes. He eased backward, dropping his hand from her face, threading his fingers through hers instead.

"You need—" The words came out huskier than usual. He cleared his throat. "You need to figure this out on your own. I can't help you."

"Why?" Her own voice was thin and breathy. On instinct she squeezed his hand, trying to anchor herself amid her spinning thoughts.

"I'm not impartial."

Excitement and dismay fought for supremacy in her mind. How long had she waited for a man like Jonah—her whole life? She'd dated some okay men along the way, even had a relationship or two, but she'd never been able to describe her romantic life as more than fine.

Now he was right here, within reach. Smart, honest, funny, sincere—her laundry list of ideal male qualities, plus gorgeous and Jewish to boot.

But that was the problem—he was *here*. And she needed to be anywhere else.

"I understand." Slowly she withdrew her hand, the absence of his touch a new, palpable loss to add to the many she already carried, and another one from which she may never recover.

They both stood, looking anywhere but each other for a silent, awkward beat.

"You'll make the right choice," Jonah said finally.

"I hope so. And if I don't, I can always come back, right?"

Jonah didn't respond—he didn't have to. They both knew that if she left, it would be for good.

He straightened his shoulders. "I'll put the boxes in the storage room."

"I appreciate it. I'll hang the posters in the lobby. Can you lock up?"

He nodded. "See you later."

A promise, not a question. She smiled. "Later."

Tonight they'd meet in their windows and light the candles for the sixth night of Hanukkah. For now, though, they turned and went in opposite directions, the space between them increasing with every step.

Chapter Twelve

*B*LEEP BLEEP. *BLEEP bleep.*

Ellie scowled at the phone on her desk. She suspected its dull, electronic-sounding ringtone had been specifically designed to be polite yet insistent, and in that moment she would've happily strangled its inventor.

She answered, explained to her colleague how to file an expense report for at least the fifth time, then switched over to another call that came through while she'd been on the line. She hung up and turned back to her computer, trying to focus on the spreadsheet on the screen.

Bleep bleep. Bleep bleep.

Ellie muttered an expletive under her breath, then answered the call in an upbeat, cheery voice. How would she get anything done at this rate? She was already behind due to taking so much time out for rehearsals. Tomorrow night was the play, and they'd given the kids today off so they'd be fresh for the performance. She'd probably be here until midnight working through the mountain of tasks she'd neglected this last week.

She gritted her teeth as she hung up. If people would just

figure out their own problems and let her do her work…

Ring ring. Ring ring.

Now it was her cell phone. Her sister's number flashed on the screen. She snatched it up with an exasperated sigh.

"Hey Naomi, I'm absolutely slammed. What's up?"

"Do you know what time you'll be home tonight?"

"Late. Why?"

Her sister paused. "We're lighting the yahrzeit candle for Mom at sundown."

Ellie cringed all the way from her gritted teeth to her clenched toes. The anniversary of Mom's death. How could she have forgotten?

Because you wanted to forget, whispered a harsh, insistent voice deep inside her head.

She glanced at the date on her computer screen, then closed her eyes as an awful, lightning-fast slideshow of memories flashed through her mind. The doctor's sympathetic, sad smile. The nurses' hushed exchanges as they came in and out of the room. The constant, silent stream of tears down Naomi's cheeks. Her own frantic mental pleading with God, begging desperately for a miracle even as she smiled reassuringly at her mother, nodding to tell her it was okay to go.

But there was no miracle that Hanukkah. Just as her faith taught her the soul enters the body with the baby's first breath, she was sure she heard her mother's depart on a peaceful exhale. Neither she nor Naomi spoke for a long time, not until a nurse came in to check on them. Her entrance was like a stone shattering a pane of glass, admitting a cacophony of noise and smells and movement that until that moment had been muted, ignorable.

Ellie had followed Naomi into the corridor numbly, like wading against the tide through knee-deep ocean water. Once they reached the waiting room Naomi fell into her husband's arms, sobbing, supported. Ellie hovered a few feet away, feeling like her presence was somehow intrusive, or impolite. Like she hadn't even had the courtesy to find a boyfriend so this moment would be less awkward.

If she'd known Jonah then… If they'd been together, if she'd had his strong arms, his murmured Hebrew condolence, his clear-headed authority, his bottomless heart…

"Ellie? Are you there?"

"I'm here," Ellie told her sister, fighting to make it true, to yank herself back from that dark day and into this not-much-brighter one.

"Can you get home in time?"

In time for what? To be the fifth wheel at the table, a stranger peering through the window at a tight-knit family's moment of grief? Naomi said home, but it wasn't Ellie's home at all. It was her sister's house, a temporary stop-off point, a guest room for a couple of weeks while she figured out her next move. She was a visitor, a welcome one certainly, but an outsider nonetheless.

Maybe one day she'd have a hand to hold and a shoulder

to lean on as she revisited this horrible date. She found comfort in that idea—she could be brave then. She could face this pain if she had someone at her back, ready to catch her if it all became too much.

Jonah.

His name sprang unbidden to the front of her mind, his image lighting the darkness behind her eyes. He would come tonight, if she asked him. She knew it as surely as she knew her own name.

But should she ask him?

"I'll do my best," she told her sister, sensing Naomi's growing exasperation on the other end of the line. "I'll let you know when I'm leaving, okay?"

"I guess," Naomi said grudgingly, and they hung up.

Ellie stowed her cell and turned back to her spreadsheet, but her mind was miles away and years ahead.

A life with Jonah. Did she dare even fantasize about it? Apparently yes, as her imagination spun faster and faster. She'd get the teaching job, and then a permanent contract, and she would trade the drudgery of corporate life for the inspiration, variety, and downright fun of introducing children to the magic of theater. She and Jonah would spend more and more time together—going out to dinner, taking her nephews to the playground, working on projects in his house.

Eventually he'd ask her to move in. He'd come to bed late, the scent of smoke clinging to his hair. She'd open her arms and bring him in close, soothing the day's dangers from his forehead, welcoming him home to the safe, peaceful world they inhabited, just the two of them.

Because that's what they'd build—a shared life. For the first time she'd be half of a whole. If she had a role in a local production, he'd be in the audience, grinning and clapping louder than anyone else. On her way to the grocery store she'd text him to see if there was anything special he wanted—and then choose a treat for him even if he said no. Every night they would unburden themselves to each other, piling their anvils on the table—he had an argument with his dad, she missed her mom—and then walk away from them hand-in-hand, their steps lighter, their hearts warmer.

And if it all worked out—if they found a way to pour their lives together and shake them into something new— then maybe, just maybe, he'd get down on one knee and—

Ring ring. Ring ring.

Ellie stared at her cell phone like it was alien technology. Slowly the fantasy she'd sunk into melted away and she blinked at the number on the screen.

Orchard Hill?

Orchard Hill!

She snatched up the phone, took a deep breath, and answered as professionally as she could muster. "Hello, this is Ellie."

"Ellie, it's Dana Gregson from Francis Murdoch Elementary. Am I catching you at a good time for a quick chat?"

"Of course. Sure. Go ahead." She sunk down a little in her chair, hoping the fuzzy walls of her cubicle would absorb most of her conversation.

"I appreciate you taking the time to meet with me the other day, especially since I know you only found out about the position at the last minute. Your credentials are beyond impressive, and I think your style and approach to teaching would be a perfect fit for our school. I'd like to offer you the maternity cover contract for the part-time drama teacher role, ideally with an eye to finding a permanent home for you by the start of the next academic year. How does that sound?"

Ellie forgot how to speak. Her mouth was open, she had words in her brain, but she could not figure out how to connect the two.

"Ellie? Did I lose you?"

"I'm thrilled, thank you so much for calling, I really, really appreciate the opportunity," Ellie replied in a rush, not only rediscovering the power of speech but doing so with such intensity that the words bumped into each other.

"Wonderful! So you accept?"

Ellie froze, her momentary sense of triumph at being chosen receding, leaving plenty of room for doubt to creep in its place.

Sure, she'd spent a couple of minutes in Mr. and Mrs. Jonah Spellman Fantasyland, but the woman on the phone was real—this choice was real. Is this what she wanted? To give up on Los Angeles—to move home to Orchard Hill?

She had a picture of a palm-tree-lined street tacked up in her cube, the iconic Hollywood sign visible in the background. She reached out and gingerly traced the letters, her fingertip whispering across the glossy magazine paper.

"I'd like to sleep on it," she told Dana. "I'll give you a call tomorrow to confirm one way or the other. Does that work?"

"Okay," Dana said, sounding surprised. "Let me know if you have any questions, otherwise we'll talk tomorrow."

Ellie thanked Dana again for the call, then put her phone down and flattened her hands on the desk, staring at the white surface between them as if the answer might magically appear there.

She wanted the job. She would love it. She would enjoy every day of it.

Except it was in Orchard Hill, where she ran into painful memories on every corner. And going back there had never been part of the plan.

Then again, neither had Jonah.

"As if that's going to work out," she scoffed under her breath, but a thin beam of optimism peeked through the darkness that had clouded her perspective since her mom passed away. She used to be exactly the sort of person who believed in romance, in happily-ever-after, and in fate. Did she really think the possibility of being happy with Jonah was more far-fetched than her Hollywood dream?

Maybe it was time to put her inner cynic to the test. If she was going to consider taking the teaching job—and that's all she told herself she had to do, simply consider—she needed the full slate of facts.

Before she could change her mind she unlocked her phone screen and tapped Jonah's number in her text messaging app.

Sooooo, I got the teaching job…

Ellie hit send and turned the phone facedown on her desk, not daring to give herself even a second to hesitate or change what she'd written. She straightened her shoulders and raised her gaze to her spreadsheet, promising herself she'd work on it for at least fifteen minutes before checking her phone. Jonah was working, anyway. He couldn't exactly stop midfire to tap out a reply.

Her phone buzzed on the desk.

Or not.

His reply was short, but every word made her heart trip disconcertingly.

Great news! Congrats!

She set her phone aside and clicked aimlessly through her spreadsheet, her thoughts whirling around her head like debris in a tornado.

Was she seriously contemplating abandoning her long-held dream—her mom's dream—of closing her fist around the stardom that slipped through her grasp when she was a kid for a future in Orchard Hill? She'd spent years trying to get away, to turn her back on a lifetime of awful memories and start over. Could one man truly be enough for her to completely reconsider?

"You're being ridiculous. This can't be about him," she murmured, raising her chin and stiffening her spine in an effort to cool her overheated mind. She couldn't let one of the biggest decisions of her life hinge on a passing infatuation with a man she'd barely known a week. This was about her career, her entire future—not a sexy firefighter with dark eyes and strong hands.

Ellie rooted through her desk and pulled out a notebook. She opened it at random, titled the left-hand page *Los Angeles*, and below it drew two columns: one for pros, one for cons. She did the same on the right-hand page, with *Orchard Hill* at the top.

Filling in the Los Angeles columns was easy. *Weather, career, adventure, excitement, fun, fresh start, new me…* She could go on and on. She bit her lip when she came to the con column, trying to be honest with herself. Eventually she jotted down *far from home* and *scary*.

The Orchard Hill page was tougher. This time she started with the cons: *Reminds me of Mom. Everyone talks about Mom. Everyone knows my sad story. Same old me, stuck in ~~the~~ my past.*

She moved over to the pros. *Naomi & family. Job. Jonah.* Short list.

She underlined Jonah's name—then added a question

mark.

Ellie propped her chin on her hands, glancing back and forth between the two pages. On paper, written in impartial black and white, the answer seemed obvious. The only true tie she had to Orchard Hill was her sister and her family, a connection easily served by visits and video chats. The temporary teaching job didn't compete with her career opportunities in California, and Jonah was an unknown quantity, their not-even-a-relationship too new and uncertain to have weight.

So why did her heart feel like it was tethered to a pendulum, swinging back and forth from here to there with no sign of stopping?

"I need a sign," she muttered.

"What's that? You need me to sign something?" Her next-door cube neighbor popped his head over the divider, eyebrows raised above his glasses.

"No, sorry, just talking to myself." Ellie offered an apologetic smile. He grinned, gave her a thumbs-up, and dropped out of sight.

Crap, I hope that wasn't the sign, because if so, I have no clue what it means. She cleared her throat and exhaled, trying for the millionth time to update this spreadsheet. She'd just wasted a good forty minutes to-ing and fro-ing over this teaching job. She'd never get back in time to light the yahrzeit candle at this rate.

She carefully typed formulas, then frowned when they

didn't work or nodded when they did. After a few minutes she was so absorbed in what she was doing that it took a couple of rings for the sound of her phone to register.

Ring ring. Ring ring.

Ellie peered curiously at her phone, then her eyes widened. She swept it up, trying hard to sound cool and casual as she answered, "Hello?"

"Ellie, it's Miles McPherson. I've got an audition for you, and I'm telling you now, you are perfect for this part. *Perfect*." Her agent never bothered with niceties. Always straight to the point.

She bolted upright in her chair. "Really? What is it?"

"Romantic comedy. Funny, poignant, couple of seriously big names attached. It'll start shooting in LA in February, but they're casting nationwide, looking for fresh faces. They can see you tonight at six thirty."

Ellie thought she might choke on the excitement clogging her throat. She asked for a sign—here it was.

"I'll be there."

"Fabulous. I'll send you the address and the pages they want you to read. Break a leg!"

She thanked her agent profusely and hung up, then pressed the phone to the center of her chest as if it were the key to a door into a magical dream world.

Maybe it was.

This meant she'd miss lighting the yahrzeit candle with Naomi and her family. Her sister would be furious.

But she would just have to get over it, Ellie decided, stowing her phone in a drawer so she could finally get some work done. She didn't have to live her life according to Naomi's rules, and her sister needed to understand that. If Naomi wanted to wallow in grief and make a big deal out of a tragedy Ellie was trying very hard to move beyond, that was her prerogative. Ellie was done with the tears, done with the sorrow. She was ready to turn her back on this horrible place and its horrible memories and start over.

Funny how that teaching job suddenly seemed a lot less appealing. And Jonah… Regret bubbled in her heart at the barest thought of him, but she had to take a chance on her dreams.

There would be other opportunities for romance. Other men with easy smiles, who listened with clear-headed sincerity, in whose eyes she saw the future rolling out before her, endless and full of promise.

There would be someone else, she told herself—but she didn't believe a single word.

Chapter Thirteen

"A LITTLE TO the left. No, not that far—okay, that's good. Maybe a bit higher?"

Jonah's arms ached under the weight of the gold-framed painting of a bearded rabbi bent over the Torah. He'd come straight to his dad's office at the end of aa long shift at the firehouse, where he'd followed up an afternoon of grueling physical training with a call to a car accident.

It had taken everything he had to keep his voice calm and soothing as he freed the sobbing toddler from her car seat and eased her through the broken glass ringing the window in the mangled rear door, then carried her over to where her mother lay on a stretcher. The reunion between the two was brief—the other driver ran a red light, smashed into the passenger side, and instantly broke the mom's right arm to the extent it required immediate surgery—but their bond was palpable, their love and relief and gratitude so intense Jonah found it hard to shake.

Afterward, while her dad gave his statement, he sat on the curb with the toddler on his knee. She sucked her thumb and rested her head against his chest, her little body warm and heavy, her hair smelling of strawberries. In that moment his postadrenaline, triumphant glow shifted, became an emptiness, an intense longing deep in his gut.

He wanted that connection. He wanted to matter to someone like this family of three mattered to each other, to anticipate seeing them during a hard day, to feel their absence, to cling to them when at last it was filled. He wanted desperately to love, and be loved in return.

And in particular, he wanted to love Ellie Bloom.

The realization arrived gently and without fanfare. He was falling for the woman who'd set her apartment on fire. Who brimmed with infectious creativity. Who practiced her faith in the hushed, dark solitude of a late-night bedroom window.

Who just might be convinced to stay in the hometown she was otherwise intent on fleeing.

"Where did I put that pencil? Hold on, Jonah—don't move."

Jonah's arms trembled as his dad rifled through his desk drawers, but he refused to complain. When his dad had texted to ask if he could help him hang pictures in his office after his shift, Jonah agreed immediately. He was exhausted, sore, and desperate to take off his boots and open a cold beer to blur the edges of this long day, but he'd greeted his father with an upbeat smile and assured him he could stay as long as the rabbi needed.

Eventually Avner crossed the room to where Jonah stood

with the painting pressed against the wall. He shoved the overturned bucket they were using as a step stool in place and hopped up, reaching across the painting to mark where they would place the nail.

"Can I put it down?" Jonah asked.

"Let me look at it one more time." The rabbi stepped back and squinted at the pencil mark for several long beats before finally nodding in satisfaction. "Perfect."

Jonah exhaled tightly as he carefully lowered the painting to the floor and propped it against the wall, then shook out his arms. "Should I get the drill?"

"Let's figure out where all of these are going before we start putting holes in the walls."

Jonah sized up the paintings arranged in a row beside the door and made a strategic move toward his father's framed degree certificates. "These should be easy. Let's get them out of the way."

He moved behind his father's desk and began ordering the degrees by date to match the way they'd hung in his old office in Boston.

The rabbi lounged against the edge of the desk, his arms folded. "The Hanukkah play seems to be coming along nicely. I'm looking forward to tomorrow's performance."

"I think everyone will like it. The kids have worked hard, and it shows."

"You know I had my doubts, but I have to admit, I've gotten wonderful feedback from the parents. It sounds like you and Miss Bloom make a great team."

Jonah smiled to himself, holding one of the frames against the wall and marking its corners. "Most of the credit goes to her. She certainly brought a lot more fun to the proceedings."

"What happened to her boyfriend? The one she was so eager to impress that she burned down her apartment?"

Jonah glanced sharply over his shoulder at his father, whose expression was vaguely curious but gave nothing away. He didn't think his dad had been listening when he told that story, and he certainly hadn't expected him to take an interest in Ellie's relationship status.

He turned back to the wall and tried to sound impassive as he replied, "Out of the picture. I don't get the impression it was serious."

"I'm surprised. She's quite a catch."

"She's moving to California." Jonah picked up the next certificate. "Maybe."

"Really? Why?"

"She wants to be an actress. She was in a movie as a kid but had to put it all on hold after her dad died. Now she's trying again. She has an agent and everything."

"That's a shame. You two would make a nice couple."

Jonah rolled his eyes as he turned to hold the second degree against the wall. "Come on, Dad, you know Mom is the family yenta. Leave the matchmaking to her."

"I'm just being honest."

Jonah hesitated, wondering whether he should say what was on his mind. He decided it couldn't hurt. "She also has a job offer here, to teach theater at the elementary school."

"Well, that certainly sounds like the better option."

Secretly Jonah agreed, but he found himself rushing to Ellie's defense. "It's the safe choice, but moving to Los Angeles has been her dream for a long time. Even if it doesn't work out in the long run, there's something to be said for going after what you really want."

Rabbi Spellman didn't respond. The silence in the room grew as heavy as the gold-framed painting, punctuated only by the light scratching of the pencil against the wall as Jonah marked the location for the second frame.

Jonah heard the creak of leather as the rabbi settled into his chair. "I take it you fully support Miss Bloom's move, then."

"Of course," Jonah said reflexively. He looked at the framed document once more, the ornate script blurring into incoherence as he saw past it to an opportunity to rebuild trust with his father. It wouldn't come naturally, but maybe this was a good chance to confide in the rabbi and call on his counsel. Show that he still respected his opinion, even if it had been a long time since he'd asked for it.

"Although I'd prefer if she stayed," he ventured, lowering the frame. Jonah pivoted to face his father, who leaned back in his chair with his hands folded in his lap.

"I can understand why. She's charming. Smart, cheerful,

full of fun—a wonderful complement to your nature."

"Which is?" Jonah asked, bracing himself for the answer.

Rabbi Spellman smiled with a fondness Jonah hadn't seen in years. "Without equal—and occasionally a little too serious."

Jonah shrugged in a gesture of sheepish accord. His dad was exactly right. Ellie brought a lightness to his often heavy, burdened spirit.

"Will you try to persuade her not to move to California?"

"I don't know. I'm not sure I have a right to interfere."

The rabbi waved his hand dismissively. "Honesty is not interference. Who knows? It might help her make a tough decision. In the end it's still her choice."

"Maybe," Jonah mused faintly, not totally convinced he had sufficient claim on her future to even venture an opinion.

"I hope she'll decide to take the job at the elementary school," Avner continued. "Teaching is exactly the sort of career you can build a life on. Steady, always in-demand, yet noble and driven by purpose. I can think of only a few professions with so much potential to provoke meaningful change in the world."

As his father spoke Jonah had slowly lowered the degree still in his hands. Now he tossed it on the table with more force than necessary, then crossed his arms, his briefly optimistic mood darkening.

"Are we talking about seminary again?"

Avner held up his hands. "I said nothing of the sort."

"Dad, we've had this discussion. I'm not going back. It's done."

The rabbi huffed in exasperation, straightening in his chair. "Can you blame me for being disappointed, Jonah? You could've been the third generation to be ordained, and you would've been the best of all of us. You have such a remarkable capacity for theological thought. I hate to see you throw it away."

"I'm sorry you perceive the daily business of saving lives as throwing away—"

"You know that's not what I mean," Avner interrupted, his tone sharpening. "If that's all you were capable of, if I didn't feel you could have even greater impact through faith, I would applaud your decision. But bandaging a wound or putting out a fire—even saving a life in an emergency—those are fleeting transactions, Jonah. One-offs. As a rabbi you could *cultivate*. You could walk people through the twists and turns of their life's journey, not just yank them back from death and then disappear."

Jonah stared at his father in disbelief, momentarily speechless. A hundred angry, outraged responses flashed through his mind, but he forced himself to stay calm. This was his father, and although it didn't always feel like it, Jonah loved him. He was committed to pulling them together, not pushing them further apart.

"I think we'll have to disagree on this one, Dad," he said

quietly, tidying the certificates into a pile. He had a feeling their picture-hanging was over for the night.

His father sighed, swiveling his chair around to face his desk. He picked up one of the framed photos arranged in a staggered formation to the left of his leather blotter. Jonah didn't have to peer over his shoulder to see which one it was—he knew. The photo showed the full four-person Spellman family standing shoulder to shoulder just outside the security line at the airport, minutes before Jonah headed off on his trip to Israel. It wasn't a great picture—they'd asked a passing stranger to take it and he'd stood slightly too far away, leaving too much floor and ceiling in the foreground. They weren't dressed up; Jonah wore a backpack. They all looked a little awkward, a little nervous, and a little excited. They were a family on the brink of a significant change, a moment as frightening as it was exhilarating.

And none of them had any idea that the oncoming change would be wildly different than what they expected.

"I hate to dredge this up, Jonah, but this time of year I can't help thinking about that phone call we got right in the middle of Hanukkah. I still don't understand what made you change your mind about being ordained."

"I told you, the fire—"

"I've heard it," Avner said agitatedly as he replaced the photo. "The fire, the lights, tikkun olam. But why not do both? Rabbis can also be EMTs, you know—neither one has to be full-time."

Jonah threw up his hands but his dad continued, "All this talk about tikkun olam, about impact—what about impact through faith? You always accuse me of not appreciating the importance of your job, but do you know my real problem with your decision? You could've been one of the great minds of Reform Judaism, but you walked away. You quit."

Jonah's grip on his temper went dangerously slack, and he pressed his palm over his eyes in a futile attempt to recover it. He took several slow, hot breaths, then lowered his hand and faced his father.

"You're right, Dad. I walked away from ordination. But I walked toward what I really wanted."

His dad scoffed. "We'll see. Who knows, maybe you'll quit this, too."

Avner pulled his laptop across the desk and clicked into his email, signaling the end of their conversation. Jonah stood, silent and motionless, the three feet separating them feeling more like three thousand miles.

On some shallow, surface level of his intellect he could dismiss his dad's criticism, telling himself it wasn't personal, just his father's way of working through his son's unexpected pivot away from his own much-loved career. With time— lots of time—he'd get over it and they would both move on.

But elsewhere, in the place where his blood hummed and his heart pulsed and air eased in and out of his lungs, he hurt. There he felt the hot shame of failure, the stomach-twisting humiliation of disappointing the man whose opinion had always been his north star.

If he couldn't make his father happy, could he ever make anyone happy? Did he even deserve to be happy himself?

He shook his head sharply, trying but not really succeeding in dispelling those ugly thoughts. Weariness came over him like a wave, and he was overtaken by a sudden, consuming need to be anywhere except exactly where he stood.

"We can finish hanging these tomorrow afternoon, before the Hanukkah performance. I'm off duty until Friday morning."

Rabbi Spellman grunted noncommittally, gaze glued to the screen.

Jonah took a last, lingering look at the man whose approving smile once had the power to warm him faster than a midsummer sun. In his place sat a veritable stranger, someone Jonah barely understood.

His entire life used to orbit around his father. Now they swung along increasingly distant routes, rarely intersecting, moving further apart with every rotation.

Jonah knew that diverging onto his own path wouldn't be easy.

He never expected it to be so lonely.

Jonah rounded the desk and plucked his jacket from the hook on the back of the door, not bothering to glance his father's way as he shrugged it on. He knew his dad wouldn't look up from his laptop as surely as he knew he wouldn't say goodbye, either. Right now Jonah existed to him only as a disappointment, an embodiment of his failures as a father, a glaring mistake he was in no mood to address.

Jonah zipped his jacket and took his car keys out of his pocket. Resignation dulled his wounds for the moment, but he knew that would change when he got home. The space and quiet would offer nowhere to hide, and he'd have no choice but to sit with this pain.

Maybe he'd just go straight to bed.

He pushed the door open and stepped through, calling over his shoulder, "Bye, Dad."

He didn't bother waiting for a reply.

Chapter Fourteen

ELLIE TURNED THE key in the lock with agonizing slowness, then pushed it open, cringing at each tiny creak. The audition ran much later than she expected, and the clock on her dashboard showed a quarter to eleven when she finally parked in front of Naomi's house. She knew her sister and brother-in-law would've just gone to bed after the ten o'clock news, and she didn't want to rouse them when they would both be up early for work the next morning.

Just common courtesy on her part—nothing at all to do with a desperate desire to avoid her sister, who was undoubtedly less than pleased with Ellie's failure to get home in time to light the yahrzeit candle.

Ellie crept across the house, taking care to step over or around the most ill-mannered floorboards. She felt her way into the pitch-black kitchen, groped for the handle of the refrigerator and pulled it open, blinking into the sudden glare of its brightly lit interior. She'd only managed a handful of cashews from the stash in her desk on her way out of the office, and now that the excitement of the audition had receded her stomach howled with hunger. She sized up the options, then reached for a packet of deli turkey and a block of cheddar cheese. She stuck a jar of mayonnaise in the crook of her arm and—

"Hey."

Ellie started, nearly dropping her armload of food as she spun. She found her sister sitting at the empty kitchen table, illuminated by the rectangular light from the refrigerator—and by the yahrzeit candle placed in front of her.

"You almost gave me a heart attack," Ellie chided, heaping the food on the counter and closing the fridge. "Why are you up so late?"

"I was waiting for you," Naomi said simply.

"I swear you weren't there a minute ago."

"I had to move the candle—I was worried the draft in the dining-room window would blow it out. Let's leave the light off—I don't want the kids to come down and think it's hangout time."

Ellie nodded. The yahrzeit candle was bright enough, bathing the room in a warm, hushed glow.

"So, how was it?"

The question she'd been dreading since she left the hotel conference room where the audition was held.

"Amazing," she answered swiftly, just as she'd planned on the drive home. "I got the part."

"Really? I didn't think they would tell you right there and then."

"Neither did I, but the casting director said I was perfect.

His team emailed the contract to my agent while I was putting on my coat."

"Wow," Naomi said, sounding as shocked as Ellie still felt. "That's great."

"It is," Ellie agreed, forcing a stiff grin. She took out a plate and two slices of bread and focused on making a sandwich. Her hand moved uncertainly, the knife glinting in the candlelight, and for a moment everything was so surreal she wondered if this was an anxious dream—if she would wake up to find, to her relief, that there was no audition, and her looming decision about leaving Orchard Hill hadn't gained a sudden, overwhelming urgency.

The knife slipped from Ellie's hand and hit the marble with a clatter. Ellie briefly closed her eyes, then opened them again.

Definitely not a dream.

"Go on, tell me about the part," Naomi prompted as Ellie slid into the seat across from her.

Ellie took a bite of her sandwich, buying time.

"It's small," she said finally. "Very small. Just a few lines in two scenes, but it's played opposite one of the stars so I guess they wanted to get it right."

"Well, you know what Mom always said. There are no small parts, only small actors. What's the character?"

"She's the lead's executive assistant. The heroine is a big-shot lawyer who falls for her rival in a divorce case. At the beginning she's really rude to her assistant, and then at the end, when she's learned lessons about love and compassion, she apologizes and is nice to her. Brings her coffee, actually."

"That's fantastic. Exactly the foot in the door you were hoping for to get you started in LA. I'm really happy for you, Ells."

"Thanks," Ellie said warily. She studied her sister for any sign of the oncoming argument about missing the candle-lighting, but all she found was encouragement and sincerity.

Naomi tilted her head. "You don't seem too excited. Aren't you happy?"

Ellie took a tactical bite, asking herself the exact same question.

The answer was no. She had every reason to be ecstatic, bursting with joy—but she wasn't. Instead her chest was tight with dread, and her shoulders constantly crept up toward her ears as worry tensed the muscles from her jaw down to her lower back. From the moment the casting director clapped his hands together in delight she'd been on the verge of tears, yet she didn't dare let the smile slip from her face, not even in the privacy of her car.

This is what you wanted, she'd reminded herself harshly, over and over again, hoping at some point the message would break through this strange wall of doubt and let triumph come rushing through. But her uncertainty only grew, and as she met her sister's gaze over the yahrzeit flame, it took every ounce of her strength not to dissolve into a blubbering heap.

"I don't think it's sunk in yet," Ellie hedged. She pushed away her half-eaten sandwich, suddenly not at all hungry. "Also."

"Also?"

"I got the job at Francis Murdoch. The principal called this afternoon. I have to give her my decision tomorrow."

Naomi tried valiantly to hide it—and Ellie's heart surged with love for her sister that she'd make such an effort to conceal her reaction—but Ellie caught the flash of hopeful delight in Naomi's eyes.

"You've got quite a decision to make," Naomi said evenly.

"No, I don't. I'm moving to Los Angeles," Ellie said firmly, ignoring the way those words seemed to make the ground shift beneath her feet.

"You're sure?"

"I've wanted to do this for a long time. Since I was a child. This is my chance. I'm going to take it."

"What about the job at Francis Murdoch?"

"It's only a part-time, maternity-cover contract. Even if I didn't have this movie role, it wouldn't be enough to keep me here."

Hearing herself put it like that, clearly and out loud, eased some of the tension clutching her body. There was no real debate here—this was apples and oranges, apples that were shiny and ripe and the oranges withered and starting to rot.

"Why did you bother going to the interview, then?"

Because she'd flirted with the idea that she might be able to assemble enough happiness—a less stressful job, time to pursue her acting, a man with broad shoulders and a quick wit—to smother the sorrow that wrapped around her every time she crossed the invisible border into Orchard Hill. That if she swapped and rearranged and adjusted, it all might add up to something big enough to make her home her *home* again.

Now it felt like a fool's errand, while the stakes had just risen sky high. In six months' time she might be miserable, but she could be miserable and unemployed in a town where the past constantly nipped at her heels, or she could be miserable under the California sun with her movie-role check in her bank account and the daily possibility that tomorrow might be better.

"I guess I shouldn't have," she told her sister. "It came up at such short notice, I didn't have time to think it through. My plan is my plan. I shouldn't have gotten distracted by a job."

Or a man.

"Well," Naomi said flatly, brushing nonexistent crumbs from the surface of the table, "we'll miss you, but we're happy for you."

Her sister's seamless shift into the collective shot iron into Ellie's resolve. She sat up straighter, leaning into her indignation, ignoring the burst of pain at her center.

"That's the thing you don't get, Naomi. You can say 'we.' You have a family—a husband, two super kids, a house with your name on the deed. I'm still looking for my 'we,' but for now I'm all I have, and it's past time I did something for myself, for my own happiness. I'm sorry if that's not what you—"

"I haven't said a word," Naomi interrupted sharply, her eyes bright with anger. "I've never so much as widened my eyes at your plan to move to LA, or your hatred of the town where I'm raising my children, or your almost total withdrawal from your family. You're finally ready to leave? Then go. But don't pretend I've ever stood in your way."

Ellie stared at her sister, fighting through the sense of having been struck to process what she'd just heard. "Is this about lighting the candle tonight? Because—"

"Of course it's not about that." Naomi threw up her hands in exasperation. "Don't you get it? All I want for you—all Mom ever wanted for you—is happiness. I don't personally understand why you need to go thousands of miles away to find it when you have people who love you right here in this house, but I'll support you, and I would never try to stop you. I just want you to... Never mind."

"Tell me. Please, Naomi—we never talk like this. Say what you're thinking."

Her sister looked up at her with a fierce expression.

"Be honest with yourself. If you get to LA and it doesn't work, or it's not what you expected... If you're unhappy, come home."

"I will," Ellie reassured her.

"I'm being serious."

"So am I."

"Promise."

Ellie hesitated. She'd never been good at admitting defeat.

"I promise," she said finally, and meant it.

Naomi nodded once, curtly, and then got up from the table. Ellie stood too, grabbing her sister's wrist to stop her, not ready to let this moment pass without sharing her own bit of truth.

"I'm sorry I haven't been around much since Mom died. Sometimes it was work, but mostly, I've been avoiding this place. I see her everywhere and…" Ellie's voice broke, tears brimming in her eyes.

"I know," Naomi said softly.

Their gazes locked. Naomi's eyes were so like their mom's, for a minute Ellie could almost believe she was here, the three of them reunited for just an instant on this grim anniversary.

As if on some silent signal, they both opened their arms and wrapped each other in a tight hug. Ellie closed her eyes and breathed in the scent of her sister's hair, letting warmth of Naomi's body seep into her own. She thought of their mom, the image so vivid she could've sworn she could smell her perfume, hear the rustle of her clothes as she moved in to join their embrace.

Their grip on each other eased and they were alone in the kitchen. Sisters without a mother. Two women abruptly elevated to the top of their family tree, still reeling from the climb, breathless from the change in altitude.

"Don't forget about us when you're rich and famous." Naomi's smile was only half-joking.

"Are you kidding? I'm counting on Gideon to be my red-carpet escort."

"Deal. Now get some sleep. You've got the Hanukkah play tomorrow. We'll talk more this weekend."

Ellie nodded, lifting one hand to say good-night as her sister made her way out of the kitchen and up the stairs.

Once she heard Naomi's footsteps upstairs Ellie dropped back into the chair at the table, looking guiltily at her barely touched sandwich. Their mom hated to waste food.

The yahrzeit candle flickered where it sat, making abstract, amber-colored shapes dance on the table's surface. Outside the circle of light the kitchen was cold and dark, but the candle's flame seemed to warm everywhere it touched.

That was Mom, Ellie thought, smiling despite the fresh tears welling at the corners of her eyes. She hoped her mom would be proud of her, landing a role in a big Hollywood movie, never abandoning her dream even though it had been years in the making.

Because it *was* still her dream—wasn't it? That sense of unsteadiness, like walking the deck on a ferry during a rough crossing, began to resurface.

She was afraid. That was it—this wasn't doubt, it was fear. That's why she hadn't been excited when the casting director offered her the part, and why her stomach twisted right now as she thought about it. Of course she was scared—she was about to leave everything she knew for a place she'd never been, to take on a career that could fail as spectacularly as it might succeed.

She exhaled slowly, her breath momentarily pushing the flame in the opposite direction. Her mom would've celebrated with her tonight. She would've tugged the cork out of whatever wine bottle had been sitting on the counter for days and gotten down the good crystal glasses, the ones normally reserved for Rosh Hashanah. She'd fantasize about Ellie's future, start working through the logistics of the move, and probably get a little teary about how happy Ellie's dad would've been. Afterward Ellie would've gone to bed, heavy-headed with wine and love and belonging.

Mom would've loved *Jonah.*

Ellie sat bolt upright, suddenly overcome by prickling urgency. Never mind where that random thought had come from—she'd missed lighting the candles with Jonah. Was he waiting for her? Did he think she'd forgotten?

She stretched a piece of cling wrap over her plate and stuck the sandwich in the fridge, then took out her phone and tapped out a text.

Sorry, just got home. See you at the window?

She took one last look at the yahrzeit candle, this time from the darkness well outside its lit circle. Then she grabbed the strap on her purse, picked up her phone with her other hand, and headed upstairs.

JONAH OPENED HIS eyes, vaguely aware of his phone chirping with a new text message. Progressively he became aware that he was slumped on the couch, fully clothed, the TV on, his neck sore and stiff. He blinked out of sleep, rubbing the base of his skull, and picked up the phone where he'd tossed it on the cushion.

Ellie.

Fully awake, he hauled himself to his feet and yawned, stretching his arms out to the sides. He'd driven home from his dad's office on a wave of disappointment, anger, and resentment, but by the time he'd kicked off his boots, stuck a frozen enchilada in the microwave, and popped the cap on a bottle of beer, he was drained of everything except weariness. Judging from what remained in the bottle, he must've dozed off within minutes of hitting the couch.

Now he had an emotional hangover. The recollection of his exchange with his dad throbbed in the center of his mind, still too tender to probe or expose to the light. He didn't want to think about any of that tonight.

He switched off the TV and ran his hand through his

hair. He tipped what was left of the beer into his mouth and carried the bottle through to the kitchen, where he tossed it in the recycling bin. He looked at the dishes in the sink, then promised himself he'd do them first thing in the morning. Then he switched off the light and started up the stairs, still creaky despite the ugly, patterned red carpet that had cloaked them for longer than he'd been alive.

When he got to his bedroom, he instinctively reached for the light, then dropped his hand.

That wasn't how this worked.

He saw her from across the room, a gray shape against a pitch-black background, edges soft and blurred on the other side of two sets of windowpanes. As he moved nearer he made out her strawberry-blond hair tossed over one shoulder, the glint of her menorah on the sill, and finally her smile, eager and friendly and…nervous?

He took his place by the window with a wave and set to the task of seating eight candles—seven for the seventh night, plus the shamash—into their holders. He hadn't cleaned out the leftover wax from last night so a couple of the candles were a tight squeeze, but after a minute or two he was ready. He looked up to see Ellie's identical effort and her waiting expression.

For the seventh night in a row they moved in silent harmony, lighting the match, letting the wick of the shamash take the flame. He murmured the blessing as their hands moved in concert, lighting one candle, and then another, and then another.

Jonah forced his thoughts away from the day's trials, away from his exhaustion and lingering disorientation, and onto the miracle of Hanukkah. The might of the righteous few against the corruption of the many. The persistence of faith and its reward. The unparalleled blessedness of having claim to this legacy, of holding a place in the Hebrew lineage, and the weighty, welcome responsibility of the future.

When he replaced the shamash candle, he felt more serene than he had all day. Never mind the situation with his dad, he still had a lot to be thankful for. A good job, a house of his own, and a woman he was rapidly falling for, presently smiling at him from behind her own blazing menorah.

Now that she was taking the job at the school, he had a real chance to turn this infatuation into something more. He'd been toying with the idea of telling her after the play tomorrow. Nothing grand, just a quiet word after everyone else had left and they were alone. He'd ask her to dinner, maybe, or breakfast this weekend, and signal that he was interested in being more than her friend. With any luck, she'd feel the same.

Who knew—he might even get a kiss.

He grinned, confidence and optimism buoying his mood. Tomorrow would be a big day—a good day.

He raised his palm to say good-night, but Ellie shook her head, holding up one finger to stall him. She carefully shifted her menorah to one side, then hauled open the window.

He did the same, sliding the brass menorah slowly so as not to dislodge the eight candles. Then he flicked the clasp on the ancient, single-pane sash window and eased it up, the wooden frame groaning in protest.

"Hi." Ellie leaned forward, resting her arms on the sill. The night was freezing but still, the air dry and unmoving, and her voice carried across the short distance as clearly as the crisp ring of a silver bell.

"Busy day?"

"Very, but good, too. I got some great news."

Even better than the teaching job? It really had been a red-letter day for her, and he smiled, happy she was happy. "Tell me."

Did her smile falter? It was hard to see her properly in the darkness, but as he squinted he was sure—

"I got a part in a Hollywood movie. I had the audition after work and they gave it to me on the spot."

His smile hung on through his surprise, but as the gears in his mind began to turn, processing what she was telling him, he felt it slipping.

"Wow. That's—wow."

"I know. It starts shooting in February. In Los Angeles. I'm moving there in a couple of weeks. It's really happening, Jonah."

He heard the slight note of pleading in her voice, her need for his approval, his blessing.

He should do the right thing. The magnanimous thing. He should be encouraging. Congratulatory. Tacitly assure her she was making a wonderful decision. Push down his true feelings and be there for her when she needed him.

Except he didn't want to, dammit.

"That's great, Ellie." The words came out flatter than he'd wanted, but it didn't matter. In a couple of weeks she'd be gone for good, and whatever designs he had on their future would be nothing more than an embarrassing memory.

He forced a smile that probably looked as thin and insincere as it felt, but it was all he could muster given the impotent, irrational anger brewing in his chest. What kind of idiot even dared imagine a woman would derail her long-held plans for a man she barely knew? His dad was right. He always let himself get carried away with big ideas, impossible ideas. When would he learn to keep his feet on the damn ground?

"Are you happy for me?" she asked, the uncertainty plain in her tone.

"Sure. This is what you wanted, right?"

"It is," she told him firmly. "It's just—my sister didn't seem thrilled, either. This is a big jump for me, and it would be nice to have a little support."

"Did your sister tell you not to go?"

Ellie shook her head. "Not at all, just made me promise to tell her if I'm unhappy out there."

"That sounds pretty supportive to me."

Ellie's smile was long gone. She'd straightened and was twisting her fingers together in front of her stomach, her elbows pointing out on either side.

"I wanted someone to be excited for me, I guess."

Jonah exhaled heavily, the last ropes tying down his irritation snapping abruptly.

"I don't know what else you want from me, Ellie. Congratulations on the part. Good luck with the move. Hopefully whatever you're running from here in Orchard Hill won't catch up with you."

She dropped her hands to the sill with a slap, brows drawn together in annoyance. "I'm not running from anything."

"I think you are," Jonah countered, the pieces coming together with sudden, perfect clarity. "I think you're running from your grief over your mom's death. That's why you bury your head in a job you hate, telling yourself lies about this imaginary life in LA where everything will be so much better—where you'll finally be happy."

"That's ridiculous," she retorted. "You're the one who told me to go after my dream. You encouraged me."

He arched his brows. "So it's my fault?"

"There is no fault. It's a plan, *my* plan, and—"

"And now that I know you better, I can see through it. I'm sorry I encouraged you to run away from your grief. There, does that fix everything?"

"What's your problem tonight?" she demanded, her voice sharp with fury. "I thought you were a decent guy, someone I could talk to. Someone who would actually listen."

Guilt punctured his anger like a rusty nail in a tire. She was right. He'd let his selfishness get the better of him, lost his temper—

"And you're one to talk about running," Ellie continued hotly. "You followed your dad halfway across the country trying to get his approval. You tell me that moving won't change how I feel—has it changed your relationship with your dad? Or was it not the magical fix you were expecting, either?"

Jonah rocked back on his heels, her words landing as squarely as a punch between the eyes. She was dead on target. He'd run toward his pain as desperately as she was running away from hers.

"It made everything worse," he admitted hoarsely, gripping the windowsill with both hands. "And it'll be the same for you."

He looked up at her, their gazes locking. "If I had a family half as loving as yours, Ellie, I'd never leave them."

Each word seem to rip out of the fabric cloaking his heart, the tightly hewn lies he'd wrapped around it in a frantic attempt to protect himself from the truth. As he spoke out loud, though, every word left a ragged, frayed-edged hole through which icy, bleak reality seeped in.

He'd turned his whole life upside down to be near his father, and it hadn't worked. He'd wasted all that time and effort and money for nothing. His dad might never love him the way he used to. The relationship he yearned to rebuild was probably gone forever.

Cold flooded his body, breaching his last defenses, chilling him from fingertips to toes.

He shivered.

Ellie was staring at him, wide-eyed, her lips slightly parted, as if she'd just witnessed an insurmountable betrayal. Then she came to life all at once, her hands rising to the window.

"Goodbye, Jonah."

She slammed the window shut, the gust of air blowing out every candle in her menorah. She swept the curtains closed, leaving him the sight of the extinguished wicks, gray plumes of smoke curling upward from each one.

He stood still for a moment, watching the smoke's receding, hypnotic spirals. He left his own window open despite the chill and drew the menorah back across the sill to the center.

The candles had burned down, but the flames were strong. He eyed them bitterly, now completely devoid of any of the hope or optimism or stalwart faithfulness they were supposed to inspire.

He was angry and fed up, and full of self-loathing for the way he'd argued with Ellie. No wonder he was alone. One minute he's planning a romantic declaration of intention, the next he's throwing emotional hot coals in the poor woman's face.

He scrubbed his hand over his face, the mere thought of what he'd said to her making him cringe with humiliation.

"What an asshole," he muttered.

His dad didn't love him, not really. He cared for him out of obligation, as a parent does, but he didn't love the man Jonah had become.

If his own father couldn't love him, why on earth did Jonah expect anyone else would?

Jonah looked down at the menorah, eight flames still flickering, bright and hot. Suddenly an icy gust of wind swept through the open window, fierce enough to make him wrap his arms around his chest as the curtains billowed and the bedroom door slammed shut.

The wind died as instantly as it swelled, like a strange, frigid sigh.

Jonah reached across the menorah to shut the window, but it was too late.

All the candles had blown out.

Chapter Fifteen

"ELLIE? ELLIE. ELLIE, this is mission control, do you read?"

Ellie jerked from her reverie with a start. Her colleague Craig had his hip propped against the side of her cubicle, his arms folded, wearing a slight smirk.

"Caught you daydreaming, huh?"

That was the last word she'd use to describe the mental contortions that had been tying her up in knots since her conversation with Jonah the night before. She'd barely slept and had spent the morning in a daze, sunk so deeply into her thoughts that she struggled to engage with the world around her beyond the most basic level.

Even now she saw Craig as if through a long, narrowing tunnel that muffled and distorted his voice on its way to her ears.

She squinted up at him. "Something like that. What's up?"

Craig launched into a tale about how his failure to reset his password on time had led to a host of problems. Ellie nodded occasionally, letting him rant, not listening to a word he said.

Instead she was back at her window, reliving the moment she told Jonah she was leaving, watching his expression shift from shock to a combination of hurt and dismay so palpable she could feel it even now, a cold knife shoved between her ribs, as surprising as it was horrifying.

He tried to conceal it, but in that instant she knew Jonah felt more for her than friendship. She tried to put his anger in that context, and although his words hit her with the force only truth can wield, she forgave him his temper. She would've reacted the same way if their roles were reversed.

If the man she was falling for—because she was falling for him, with the terrifying speed and steep angle of a drop on a rollercoaster—told her he was about to walk out of her life for good.

"Ellie? Have you heard a word I've said?" Craig's mouth pulled down in exasperation.

"I did. Sorry, I've got a lot on my mind today. You need to call Pete in IT, he can fix it."

"Thanks, Els," he said cheerfully. Craig turned and had even taken a few steps away from her cubicle when he looked back, his expression sheepish and reluctant, like he knew he should ask this question but he didn't really want to invest the time the answer would require. "Everything okay with you?"

"Fine. Actually…" She made a sudden, drastic decision. Craig couldn't keep a secret if his life depended on it.

Anything she told him would spread around the office like wildfire. That might make what she had to do today easier, if she didn't have to tell everyone individually.

And if everyone already knew, she couldn't chicken out and change her mind.

"I got a part in a movie. I'm finally moving to LA. Don't tell anyone," she whispered, knowing those three words would guarantee this fact would soon reach every set of ears on this floor—and a few on the floor above.

Craig opened his mouth in exaggerated surprise. "Wow, Ellie, congratulations! Don't worry, my lips are sealed." He drew his fingers across his mouth as if zipping them.

"Thank you. I'm excited." She managed to smile—she was a talented actress, after all—and Craig hurried away much faster than his first attempt. Clearly a juicy morsel of gossip was more urgent than his malfunctioning computer.

She swiveled back to her own screen. Seven new emails had accumulated in the time she'd spent speaking to Craig. She clicked on the first one but the words blurred in her vision, and for the life of her she just didn't care what it said.

Soon there would be an increasingly indiscreet stream of people stopping by her cubicle to verify the rumor of her imminent departure. Time wasn't on her side, so she'd better do what she needed to do.

She opened a blank document and began to type her resignation letter.

The words came easily enough, thanking her boss for

their years working together, appreciating that he'd taken a chance on her when she had no background in banking. However an opportunity had arisen—she didn't specify exactly what—that was too good to pass up, so please consider this her formal notice, blah blah blah.

She reread it quickly, then printed it out and signed in blue ink.

"That was the easy part," she murmured, spotting a couple of heads popping up over their cubicles to look at her.

Now she had to go through with it.

Ellie rose from her chair and began the slow walk to her boss's corner office on unsteady feet. She'd fantasized about this day since her first week on the job, but she didn't feel any of the elation or freedom she'd imagined. And unlike her dreams of this moment, it wasn't the choice to quit that worried her—it was what might come next.

She paused outside his glass door, clutching the letter. He was on the phone, but gestured for her to wait, and after a few seconds he hung up and motioned her inside.

"Do you have a minute?" she asked.

"Of course. What can I do for you?" He indicated the deep leather chairs in front of his desk, and she took a seat.

"This was such a tough decision, but unfortunately I'm handing in my notice," she said, passing him the letter as she spoke.

He read it briefly, then met her gaze with a resigned smile. "I'm sorry to lose you. You know I think you're fantastic, but I know we've been a little slow in offering you much in the way of career progression. May I ask where you're headed? If it's another bank, perhaps we can—"

"Los Angeles."

His brows rose above the thin rims of his glasses. "That's a big change. I guess you're finally getting back to the acting?"

"Yes. Finally," she echoed with a tight smile.

"Well, I wish you nothing but success. Of course you know the bank's policy—given our access to highly confidential materials, we ask all of our departing employees to leave immediately and serve their notice from home."

Ellie nodded. She knew. In fact she'd already made plans to use the rest of the day to wrap up preparations for the Hanukkah play and generally try to steel herself to see Jonah that evening.

"Considering you've been such a valued member of the team, however, on this occasion I'll make an exception. Why don't you take an hour or two to arrange a handover? Then you can have a long, leisurely lunch, and we'll celebrate your time with us this afternoon. You can turn in your badge afterward. How does that sound?"

She knew he was trying to be gracious and give her the recognition he felt she deserved. Part of her was flattered and grateful.

The rest wanted to wring his neck.

"Perfect. Thank you for being so understanding."

They concluded a few work-related loose ends and then Ellie stormed back to her desk, where three of the office's worst gossips hovered beside her cubicle.

By the time she'd explained the situation several times to successive waves of visitors to her desk, Ellie's confidence in her decision had risen substantially. Hearing herself describe it out loud—the big names attached to the movie, the doors this role could open, the rare luck of arriving in LA with a job already in hand—tipped the nauseatingly shifting seesaw of her thoughts back toward Hollywood and the dream that if she could just get there, everything else would work itself out.

In moments she even laughed loud enough to drown out Jonah's voice in her head.

Hopefully whatever you're running from here in Orchard Hill won't catch up with you.

She ignored her lingering unease, rapidly typed up a handover document, then grabbed her coat and fled the office before anyone could stop her.

She burst out of the lobby into the bitterly cold December day, the noon sun weak and already starting to dip, yet she was invigorated. She stood on the plaza taking full, icy lungfuls of air, every muscle in her body easing as she realized what she'd just done.

She'd quit.

Ellie tilted her face toward the thin sunshine and closed her eyes, allowing herself a moment of sheer bliss. She'd just walked away from one of her biggest sources of misery, a job she hated and a salary that kept her handcuffed to the status quo. No matter what happened next, she was proud of herself for taking this step—and grateful to Jonah, who'd shown her that quitting was not the same as failing, and that sometimes it was the best choice to make.

Jonah. She opened her eyes and tightened the top of her coat against the intrusive touch of an icy breeze.

She had time to kill before returning to the office for the last time to attend her farewell party, so she took a seat on the broad edge of a planter, made from the same smooth, polished granite as the floors in the lobby. Ellie turned her back to the wind and watched a group of workmen build some sort of bronze-colored metal structure at the front of the plaza.

Watching these men work with their hands, expertly twisting screws and helping each other lever heavy-looking bars into place, her thoughts returned to Jonah. His passion for action, his sincerity about his tikkun olam, and the way he turned his life upside down so he could be elbow-deep in impact.

There was no denying it—she'd fallen for him like a grand piano tumbling out of a twentieth-story window, and landed just as messily, with a crash that could be heard for miles.

But what they'd said to each other last night, the barbs they'd hurled—could either of them ever get over it?

And if she was leaving in a matter of weeks, did it matter?

One of the workmen paused, brushing his hands on his coveralls as he stepped back to survey the work-in-progress. Her curiosity must've shown in her expression, because he looked over at her, and then smiled.

"It's a menorah. For Hanukkah. The property company that owns the building is trying to be a little more inclusive with their holiday decorations."

"Hanukkah ends tonight. It's been going on for a week. Why'd they wait until the last night to put up a menorah?"

He shrugged. "Better late than never?"

"What they missed in timeliness they're making up for in size, I guess."

"Tell me about it." He shook out his arms. "Do you celebrate Hanukkah?"

She nodded.

"What's it all about, really? I only know it's a Jewish holiday, and people light candles."

"Miracles," she answered. "Belief that good will always triumph. Faith amid adversity. But mostly, miracles."

He grinned. "Sounds nice."

"It is."

"I better get back to it, but be sure to take a look down here once it gets dark. Like you said, they didn't scrimp on size."

She smiled. "I will."

"Happy Hanukkah, ma'am."

"Happy Hanukkah," she echoed softly. The workman gave her a little nod and rejoined his colleagues. She watched for another minute, but then a shadow slid over the sun, plunging her spot into frigid shade. She took one last look at the half-built menorah—still just a mess of poles and panels and screws—then pushed off the planter and headed off in search of lunch.

"FOR SHE'S A jolly good fellow…which nobody can deny!"

Ellie smiled and tipped her head in gratitude as the colleagues gathered in a semicircle around her desk applauded. Her boss had already said a few complimentary—if somewhat impersonal—words about her tenure, she'd been presented with a cake topped with a mini version of the Hollywood sign, and her desk was surrounded by California-themed decorations including cardboard flip flops and an inflatable palm tree. She was flattered that so much effort had gone into such a last-minute celebration, and although she was still delighted to say goodbye to her cubicle forever, it was nice to finally get some recognition of how much she'd helped people on a daily basis.

Her boss left the impromptu party right after the song finished, but the rest of her colleagues milled around, grateful for an excuse to step away from their desks. Ellie answered questions about the film and her move with a cheerful smile, despite the kernel of doubt that lodged in her throat and made her feel like she'd swallowed a peppermint whole.

She'd taken herself out for a long lunch, trying and failing to forget that she still owed the principal at Francis Murdoch a call, and ignoring the film contract sitting unread in her email inbox. She repeatedly told herself that Los Angeles was a foregone conclusion at this point, and the only decisions still to be made were about flight times and apartment leases. As for Jonah, well, it might be awkward during the Hanukkah play tonight, but after that she never had to see him again. Soon he'd be out of sight, out of mind.

She sighed around a piece of Hollywood sign-shaped cake, remembering her lunchtime mental spiral. She'd never been a good liar, especially to herself.

But that wasn't quite true, was it?

Jonah's words echoed in her head, getting louder and louder as the day had worn on. Maybe she'd been lying to herself for years—insisting that she was running toward her dream in LA, not fleeing from her grief here in St. Louis.

"I so admire you," one of her colleagues said, leaning against the edge of the cubicle. "I've always dreamed of blowing everything off and moving to Hawaii to teach yoga. I even did my instructor's certificate last year. With my savings I could make it work, I really could, but I know myself—I'd run home crying the first week. My whole family is here, and I would miss them way too much. I love that you're so independent. This is such a brave move, Ellie."

"I don't feel brave," Ellie blurted before she could stop herself.

"You are," her colleague assured her, but Ellie's whole being seemed to be shifting in the opposite direction. She felt terrified that she was making the wrong decision. Guilty that she was moving away from Naomi, depriving her sister of what little family she had left. Worried about whether she would really make it out there, and what would happen if she didn't. Regretful about Jonah, about the job at Francis Murdoch, about her own unwillingness to give life in Orchard Hill a chance.

Soon the party died down, and one by one her colleagues drifted back to their screens. They made her promise to keep in touch, reminded her to let them know when the movie came out, and wistfully imagined future meetups on California vacations, but Ellie knew it was unlikely she'd speak to any of them again. She picked up the empty box someone had left on her chair and began packing her things.

She'd papered her cubicle with pictures she'd hoped would inspire her to achieve her dream: the Hollywood sign, Santa Monica Pier, the Chinese Theatre, the Walk of Fame... For years she'd touched these images like talismans, connections to the future she dreamed of, but as she pulled out the pins they felt flimsy and insignificant. She organized them into a pile, then quickly realized they'd never survive the journey in the box. The slightest weight and they'd rip or wrinkle, ruined beyond use.

She tossed the whole stack into the trash.

In the end, everything she wanted to take with her fit into her purse. She left the box where she'd found it, shrugged on her coat, and pulled the lanyard holding her building ID off her neck.

No one noticed her slip out of the office for the last time, past rows and rows of people bent toward their screens. She had a momentary pang of regret—she'd had some good colleagues here, and she'd made lots of money at a time when she desperately needed it—but it vanished as soon as the elevator doors swished closed, shutting off her view of her now former workplace.

The swift descent through the skyscraper always made her feel momentarily light, like her insides hadn't quite made the journey and were racing to catch up, but this time it remained when she hit the ground floor. Her feet seemed to barely touch the floor as she crossed the lobby, handed in her badge, and stepped through the doorway toward the rest of her life.

Night had fallen while she'd been upstairs, and as she stepped away from the sheltering reach of the building a rush of wind nearly swept her off her feet, whipping past with an icy chill she felt all the way to her bones.

She hugged her arms around herself, motionless amid the hustle and bustle of people crossing the plaza.

Now what?

She should call her agent and tell him she'd be signing the contract shortly. She should call the principal at Francis Murdoch and decline the teaching position. She should text Jonah, make amends for last night, and ask if there was anything she could pick up before the performance.

Then she should walk into her hard-won, blindingly bright future in LA.

She did none of those things. Instead Ellie found herself stumbling toward the fully built but unlit menorah in the plaza, now a towering, elegant structure of bronze and glass, gleaming despite the darkness. She peered up at it, lifting her chin to see all the way to the top. The workmen did a great job. Even shadowed and dormant, it was beautiful.

Suddenly the central lamp, representing the shamash candle, flared to life. She staggered backward, awash in the radiance of the powerful bulb, gaping up at the menorah.

The right-most candle lit up. Then the one to its left. Then another, and another, the soft hum of an electrical current growing louder. One by one each of the candles flashed and then glowed, the bulbs simulating the flickering of actual flames.

By the time they were all alight, she wasn't standing in darkness anymore. She was illuminated, surrounded by brightness, the pool of light at her feet marred only by her own shadow.

That's when she heard it.

Her mom's laugh.

She didn't bother to turn around, didn't so much as glance to one side. She knew the sound had been carried on the wind of her imagination, a wish made fleetingly real.

Her favorite of her mom's laughs. Not the easy, merry one that followed a grin, or the polite but restrained one she used for strangers' children or passing chitchat. There, standing in the menorah's electric blaze, Ellie heard her unexpected laugh, the one that took her by surprise, when something was so funny or delightful or simply too wonderful to bear.

To Ellie, it was the sound of unforeseen happiness. Of an unpredicted but welcome turn of events. Of the enduring potential for joy in this bittersweet world.

Ellie began to cry.

She wept for her mother, for all of the suffering in her too-short life. She wept for herself and her sister, their rending loss, their still-sharp grief. She wept with fear, with mourning, and with hope.

When at last her head felt empty and her heart full to bursting, she wiped the tears from her cheeks and stood up straight. Tonight the celebration of Hanukkah would conclude, but its miracles would leave her forever changed.

She knew exactly what to do.

Chapter Sixteen

"ARE YOU SURE you'll be able to start on time? So many people have come, I don't want to keep them waiting. If you want, I can step out and—"

"Dad," Jonah commanded firmly. "It's fine. Ellie got hung up at work, but she'll be here any minute."

Avner shot him a skeptical glance, but walked away without another word, busying himself with something on the other side of the classroom full of excited, costumed children.

Jonah took out his phone and scowled at the blank screen. He hadn't heard from Ellie all day and he had no idea why he was covering for her.

Oh, wait, yes he did. Because he was a lovesick moron who didn't know when to quit.

All day he'd fought the urge to text her and apologize for his short temper the night before, and all day he'd resisted, telling himself there was no good outcome here. She was leaving, and she didn't need any more emotional complexity—certainly not half-baked romantic overtures from someone she'd barely known a week.

Whatever spark had briefly flared between them was gone, and it wouldn't be fair to either of them for him to keep trying to reignite it. He just had to get through the performance tonight, move his menorah away from his bedroom window, and then he'd never see her again.

Although if she didn't show for the performance, which was looking more and more likely, he supposed their ending was already complete.

"Mr. Jonah, is Miss Ellie here yet? I wanted to say my line for her one last time." Zach, now fully garbed as Judah Maccabee (if Judah Maccabee wore light-up sneakers), stood at his elbow.

"She's stuck in traffic, but hopefully she'll be here any minute. Want to say it for me in the meantime?"

"I think I'll wait for Miss Ellie. We were working on my character's emotion. Thanks anyway," Zach said with the exact tone of a parent not wanting to undermine their child's effort to help with something way out of their league.

"Let me know if you change your mind," Jonah called as Zach departed. He had to hand it to Ellie. She'd fostered incredible enthusiasm in these kids. Even the most reluctant at the beginning were now fired up, and the crowded room buzzed with energy and anticipation.

He'd already tried some of her techniques in his Hebrew classes with definite success. If nothing else, he'd take away a few pointers from her on how to connect with kids about subjects they were less than thrilled about.

Who was he kidding? He'd take way more than that. Ellie had left her mark from the moment they met, when she was a stranger stoically facing the near-complete destruction of her apartment. Her irrepressible spirit had been palpable in that smoke-stinking, scorched, dripping mess, and he should've known then and there that she was destined for a life bigger than he could ever imagine. That she'd given him any time at all should demand his gratitude. That she'd encouraged him, admired him, bolstered the sense of direction his dad's hostility constantly threatened to throw off course was more than he deserved, more than he had any right to hope for.

But he had hoped, and now he would pay the price. He didn't need his dad's anxious shuffle back across the room to tell him the performance was due to start.

No sign of Ellie, and although he felt increasingly uneasy about her absence—he simply didn't believe she would miss the play without a damn good reason—he didn't have the energy or the inclination to speculate where she might be. He'd just have to do this on his own.

"Jonah, I really think—"

"We'll start without her. I don't know what's happened, but hopefully everything's all right and she just got held up downtown. You can go get everyone seated and give your opening remarks. I'll have the kids lined up and ready."

"Great. Let's get started." His father half turned to go, then seemed to change his mind. When he met Jonah's gaze once more, his expression was different. Softer. More open.

"You've done a wonderful job with these kids, Jonah. I was speaking to some of the parents, even the kids themselves—everyone is so full of praise for you, and for everything you do for the Temple Sinai community. I know I've always held you to a high standard, and I want you to know it's only because I think you're capable of so much. I can already tell tonight's performance will be excellent. I'm proud of what you've done."

The rabbi ducked his head in farewell and quickly left the classroom, leaving Jonah staring open-mouthed at the spot where he'd just stood.

Less than twenty-four hours ago their relationship was at an all-time low. Could a few compliments from parents and kids really turn everything around?

"Hanukkah miracles never cease," Jonah muttered, then summoned the kids for a final preshow pep talk.

A few minutes later, and with only a couple of concerned questions about Miss Ellie's whereabouts—an issue he, too, was finding increasingly alarming—Jonah had the kids lined up in order of appearance along the hallway they used as a backstage area. He heard his father thanking the various community volunteers who'd helped fund or donate elements of the production, including Noa Jacob, the thrift store owner he'd spotted taking a seat in the last row of pews.

"Most of all, I'd like to thank the two people most instrumental in making this evening's performance possible:

Eliana Bloom, and my son, Jonah Spellman. Without them, this year's Hanukkah would undoubtedly have lacked the sparkle you're about to enjoy. And now, without further ado…"

Jonah barely heard the end of his father's speech, or his own whispered encouragement as he sent the first group of performers through the side door to the sanctuary. His chest was tight, his ears burned, and his head buzzed with the echoing warmth and affection in his father's words.

My son.

There were times these last couple of years when Jonah truly believed his father hated him, and that the day might come when they stopped speaking to each other altogether, maybe for the rest of their lives. He thought there was nothing he could do to shake off his father's disgust. That the man he loved and admired so intensely was lost to him, because his own happiness and his father's approval would never be compatible.

Tonight, for the first time since that faraway Hanukkah in Israel, the bright light of a tiny, hopeful flame punctured Jonah's heavy, black despair.

A tug on his sleeve jerked him back to the present, and it was like stepping out of a silent, empty room into a hurricane. A Maccabee needed to go to the bathroom. He sent her running down the hall, hoping she wouldn't miss her cue. A Temple Restorer needed help tying her shoe. A Candle Lighter had a question about where to stand. Meanwhile he tried to keep one ear on the performance so he'd know who to send out when. And where on earth was Ellie? He pulled his phone from his pocket but there was nothing. He began to type a text message. He couldn't believe that she would miss the show deliberately—something must be wrong.

Play just started, where are you? If you need

The sound of the temple's double front doors slamming open resonated like thunder down the small hallway. Jonah heard the clatter of footsteps, then another crash as the rear sanctuary doors were flung open. Inside he heard a man's voice, muffled but urgent. A Maccabee stopped talking midsentence. With a hasty instruction to the children to stay exactly where they were, Jonah slipped inside the side entrance to see what was going on.

A man in a delivery service uniform stood in the middle of the aisle, eyes wide with panic. The rabbi caught Jonah's eye and motioned him forward.

"Jonah, thank goodness. This man says there's been an accident outside. Go with him, now."

Rabbi Spellman turned to the man in the aisle as Jonah ran to join him. "My son is a paramedic. He can help."

"I called 9-1-1 but I saw the temple and thought maybe someone knew first aid," the man explained as they jogged through the lobby together. Behind them Jonah heard his father calming the congregation, imploring everyone to relax during this unexpected intermission.

"Did you see the accident?" They were crossing the parking lot now.

The man shook his head. "I came up behind the car at the intersection. Looks like a hit and run, if you ask me. There's a lady inside, but she—"

"Show me." A layer of frost seemed to knit around Jonah's heart as an unthinkable possibility pieced itself together in his mind.

He followed the man off Temple Sinai property to the intersection a block away. Accidents were common there— one of the roads was a route to a highway feeder, so hurrying drivers frequently ran the red, gambling on the comparatively light traffic crossing the other way.

The streetlights did little to penetrate the midwinter darkness, and without a coat the wind cut through Jonah's shirt, but he hardly noticed. His attention was fixed on the muted gleam of the shape on the shoulder, red taillights barely visible behind a hedge. The details of what he saw gradually arranged themselves into a whole picture. Gray sedan. Significant impact to the driver's-side door. White plume of an airbag visible through—

Ellie.

He broke into a sprint, covering the last few feet to the car faster than he'd ever run in his life. Fear was an icy fist gripping his throat but he forced himself to remain calm, inspecting the scene with clinical detachment even as his thoughts raged like a wildfire.

Who did this? How do you ram into a car hard enough to

push it off the road and just keep driving? If they find that driver—when they find that driver, I'm going to personally... But not now, now I need to focus on Ellie, make sure she's safe. If anything happens to her, if I can't save her...

He closed his eyes, slamming a mental door on that dark line of thinking, and then reopened them with as much professional objectivity as he could muster.

Ellie appeared unconscious, her head lolled to one side, albeit not at a worrying angle, and her chest rose and fell calmly. The airbag had deployed, and he couldn't make out any signs of physical injuries through the window, but he did detect the scent of gasoline. A quick glance under the chassis found a rapidly growing puddle of liquid, and the situation became significantly more urgent.

"Is she breathing?" The delivery driver had caught up to him. Jonah nodded, and he sagged with relief.

"Thank God. I was afraid I was too late."

"You saved her life," Jonah told him sincerely.

Without taking his eyes from Ellie he pulled his phone from his pocket, unlocked the screen, and handed it to the delivery driver. "Emergency services should be here any minute, but I'm worried about the fuel line damage to the car. Dial the number listed for Avner Spellman—that's my dad, the rabbi you saw at Temple Sinai. Tell him where we are, and that we need a fire extinguisher. Fast."

The man stepped back to make the call. Jonah tugged on the car door handle and was relieved to discover that it had unlocked automatically when the airbag deployed. When he eased the door open, the odor of gasoline intensified, and he immediately reached across the steering wheel to turn off the ignition. He knelt on the asphalt and, after another quick visual sweep that found no previously unseen wounds, he touched Ellie's hand where it rested on her knee.

"Ellie? Can you hear me?"

Her eyelashes fluttered against her cheeks, and then she slowly opened her eyes. She frowned, turned that bluebird gaze toward him, and, after a second's consideration, broke into the most beautiful smile he'd ever seen.

"My sexy firefighter, rushing to my rescue once again."

Jonah laughed, not only at her words, but as a release for the dizzying combination of joy and gratitude and relief and lingering fear and something else—something powerful and serious he didn't dare examine too closely right now—threatening to overpower his judgment.

"It's just me, but I'll let you know when he gets here."

"Don't be ridiculous." Ellie's voice was lazy and relaxed, as though they were picnicking on a spring afternoon and not at the scene of a car accident. "You're ten times hotter than those fires you put out. By the way, if the fire department ever does a calendar—"

"Clearly you have a head injury."

"A headache, yes, but otherwise I'm fine." She shifted gingerly in her seat, then pressed her palm to her forehead. He put his hand on her shoulder to keep her still.

"You lost consciousness, so you're almost certainly concussed. Normally I'd tell you not to move, but…" What was a less frightening way to say, *I'm worried your car is about to explode*?

"Nothing else hurts, I promise."

That didn't mean she had no internal injuries, but he had to take the chance. "We're going to do this slowly. If anything feels off, let me know."

She nodded. He eased up into a crouch and slid his arm between her back and the seat, tightening his grip around her waist. She reached across his shoulders, one hand braced just beside his neck, and he angled sideways to tuck his other arm beneath her knees.

The warmth of her body was reassuring against flesh made cold by the icy air. He felt the soft thump of her heart against his wrist, strong, steady, unhurried. He caught the sweet scent of her cutting through the acrid smell of gas, jasmine and lemon and baby powder, and when he turned his head she was already looking at him, blue eyes wide and searching and so hopeful that the air stuttered in his lungs.

"Jonah, last night I—"

Something sizzled and popped under the hood, loud enough to draw both of their attentions. As Jonah watched a thin, gray line of smoke erupted from the seam near the windscreen. A single word registered in the center of his mind, clear and hot.

Fire.

"We have to get you out of here. Now."

He tried to scoop Ellie out of the driver's seat but she cried out, her arms tightening around his neck.

"My foot is caught." She reached down, rooting in the well near her right ankle.

"There! Over there!"

Jonah vaguely took note of the delivery driver's voice calling from what sounded like across the street, but he didn't even bother to look over his shoulder. Instead he leaned over Ellie's lap, squinting into the dark space near her feet.

"Jonah, I'm stuck. I can't get out." Ellie's voice had grown thin and high with alarm. He could see her wrenching her leg to no avail, but he couldn't make out what was trapping her.

"Don't worry. I've got you," he told her with an ease he didn't feel. He hoped he wasn't lying.

This would've been a great time for the fire truck to show up with all its equipment, Jonah thought grimly. He heard the approaching footsteps of what he guessed were a handful of Temple Sinai members, but no sirens.

He'd have to figure this out himself.

He slid his hand down Ellie's stockinged calf, trying to feel his way to the problem. He grimaced in the darkness, struggling to make sense of everything his hand encountered, when he felt the line of stitching and knew exactly what had happened.

"The strap on your purse is twisted around your foot. Did you have it stashed down here?"

"No, it was on—Jonah?"

He glanced up, but Ellie stared straight ahead. He followed her line of vision.

A row of flames leaped from the seam in the hood, illuminating the car's interior in an eerie, wobbling glow.

Jonah swore viciously and set to work untangling Ellie's foot. His hands shook and his fingers felt numb and clumsy, what should have been a simple task seeming like it took hours as his thoughts careened and his heart hammered at breakneck speed.

"Not today," he muttered under his breath, fighting to steady his hands, forcing himself to methodically follow the line of the strap so he could swiftly pull it loose. Today would not be the day he lost his cool. Today would not be the day he screwed it all up. Today would not be the day he lost the woman he loved because he couldn't move his goddamn fingers fast enough.

There it was—he loved her. And at exactly the same instant that awareness soared and burst in his mind like a firework, he pulled the strap away from Ellie's ankle and freed her foot.

"Now," he shouted, all his concerns about gentleness vanishing as he resumed his grip, grabbing her tightly at her waist and knees. She wrapped her arms around his neck and leaned into him.

A spark; the groan of hot metal as it warped; a great *whoosh* as the flames on the hood roared, doubling in size.

Jonah felt the heat along the left side of his body, squinted against the sudden, bright light of the blaze. He held Ellie as tightly as he could and threw himself backward, praying it would be far enough, fast enough.

Jonah landed hard on his tailbone, the asphalt cold and unforgiving, the impact ricocheting through his bones. He clutched Ellie to his chest, watching wide-eyed as flames engulfed the front end of the car. He ignored the pain searing up his spine and shot to his feet, staggering backward, not daring to loosen even a finger as he carried Ellie to safety.

In the few minutes he'd spent pulling Ellie from the car—and it had been only a few minutes, not the year it seemed—his world had shrunk to the two of them, the ruined vehicle, and the silent but unyielding march of time. Now a hand touched his back and the world gaped wide, suddenly crowded and noisy and full of motion.

Sirens wailed as a fire engine rounded the corner, followed closely by an ambulance. A man from Temple Sinai pointed a fire extinguisher at the car from several feet away, the white discharge—wait, wasn't that Sonia's dad?

The idea of the play, of the kids, that fifteen minutes earlier he had been fixing costumes and speculating about Ellie's whereabouts seemed impossible. He blinked, trying to recover his bearings, and realized he was surrounded by people saying his name.

"Jonah, are you all right?" Another one of the dads, a doctor, squinting at his face.

"Jonah, thank God." His dad, the hand on his back.

"Jonah." A woman's voice. Shaky, a little breathless, but perfectly safe.

Ellie.

She beamed up at him. "You can put me down now."

He wanted to kiss her. Pull her even closer. Promise he'd never let anything happen to her. Tell her he loved her, and always would.

Then he remembered—she was leaving. And no matter what he felt for her, or how much he'd miss her, in a few weeks he'd be little more than a memory, an ever-blurring shape in her rearview mirror.

He lowered her to the ground.

As soon as her feet touched the asphalt Ellie was surrounded by people and ushered away, like ants carrying off a dropped crumb. Half of the play's audience had to be on the scene now, and Jonah could barely see the top of Ellie's head as she was escorted to the waiting ambulance by her sister and several other kids' parents.

Soon he was swarmed, too. He found himself mechanically answering questions from the police who'd arrived on the scene, half-heartedly talking shop with the local fire district team who'd been told he worked for the department in St. Louis, and politely acknowledging the gushing admiration of Temple Sinai congregants—more than one of whom suggested they'd love to introduce him to their daughter.

"She lives in Denver, but I'm always trying to convince her to move home to Orchard Hill. I'll let you know next time she's in town, maybe the two of you—"

Jonah didn't hear the rest of Mrs. Rubin's sentence—he was too focused on the ambulance's backup lights, which had suddenly come on. The door was closed—was Ellie inside? Were they taking her to the hospital?

"Excuse me, Mrs. Rubin, I have to go check something." He didn't wait for her reply as he set off, weaving through the throng of onlookers as quickly as he could. By the time he made it to the edge, though, the ambulance was trundling down the road.

"Is Ellie gone?" he asked the first person he saw, which happened to be his dad.

The rabbi nodded. "She went to the emergency room. She seems fine, but they'll run some tests, make sure she's okay."

Of course she'd gone, it made perfect sense, and he would've recommended the same course of action if he'd attended the scene on a professional basis.

Then why did he feel utterly bereft?

"Jonah." His father's voice drew his attention, and he found his dad wearing a grave, earnest expression.

"All day I've been thinking about our conversation in my office. Then with all the compliments from the parents on the play, and seeing you run so bravely toward danger tonight—I owe you an apology. A big one."

Jonah gaped at his father, not quite believing what he was hearing.

"I know I've always been hard on you, and I've told myself it's because you exceed every standard I set, so the best thing to do is to keep raising the bar. But that achievement-oriented approach ignores something I don't think I appreciated until now. Your happiness."

"Dad, you didn't—"

Avner shook his head, halting Jonah's interruption. "Please, let me own my error. I let myself be consumed with disappointment by your diversion from the path that I valued, and I made no space to consider the upsides, or to remove myself entirely and view the situation from your perspective. I put you through a lot of unnecessary pain, and I'm sorry. I hope you'll let me try to repair things between us."

"Of course, Dad. That's all I want. That's why I'm here."

Jonah didn't want to waste a second on doubt or indignation or skepticism. Before his father could say another word he opened his arms and wrapped him in a hug, the first embrace they'd shared since he left for Israel, since their relationship as they knew it was irrevocably changed. Avner squeezed him tightly and Jonah exhaled, releasing years of resentment, anguish, and desperation.

The past was gone. He wanted nothing more than to

seize his dad's willingness and work on the future.

"I have some responsibility in this, too," Jonah admitted once they let each other go. "I pinned my happiness to your approval, and that wasn't fair to either of us. I should've focused on myself, and instead of chasing you down here I should've followed my own path to being happy."

Exactly like Ellie was doing, he thought with a bitter-sweet pang. Following her own path.

He couldn't blame her. Even though that path would lead her far away from him.

His dad clapped him on the back. "You're here now, that's what matters. We'll fix things. I promise."

For better or worse, it was the last night of Hanukkah. He'd gotten his wish—at least part of it.

"Okay, Dad." He smiled at his father, at the prospect of a new beginning, at a life enriched by what he'd learned from Ellie, even if she wasn't part of it.

"We will," Jonah promised.

"WELL, I'M VIEWING it as a compliment. My brain is vast and complex, possibly the most intricate one known to science, and that's why these results are taking forever to come back."

"Or it's so tiny they couldn't find it on the scan." Naomi winked, passing Ellie yet another cup of watery tea.

They'd been sitting in a curtained-off square in the emergency room for nearly two hours, and with the refreshments kiosk closed for the night, one of the nurses had taken pity on them and brought a handful of herbal tea bags from the staff lounge.

"At least the hospital isn't busy tonight," Ellie remarked. "Imagine if we were competing with a retirees' bowling tournament gone wrong."

"I don't know, a few drunken senior citizens brawling over cheating allegations might liven the place up a little."

"It's still early."

"Sort of." Naomi checked her phone, then smiled and held it up, showing Ellie a picture of Gideon and Isaac in their costumes. "Are these the cutest kids you've ever seen or what?"

"Hands down. I'm so glad they were able to restart the performance. I would hate for all their hard work to go to waste."

"Shame you missed it, though."

Ellie began to shrug it off, then stopped. She'd promised herself she would start being honest with herself and everyone around her, even when it was hard—like right now.

"I'm super disappointed," she admitted instead. "I was beyond invested in this production. I know Dan recorded it, but it won't be the same."

Naomi patted her knee sympathetically. "It's too bad you couldn't see it, but it got rave reviews. I'm not sure what will keep the congregation chatting longer, Jonah's heroic rescue or the stellar Hanukkah play."

Ellie smiled, recalling the moment Jonah had pulled her free from the car, her terror instantly shifting to something far more intense and immeasurably more hopeful.

"It was pretty epic, huh?"

"Beyond. You must've been so scared, though. We can laugh about it now, but it was probably horrifying."

Ellie tilted her head, considering. "Yes and no. By the time I made sense of the situation Jonah was there, and I knew he wouldn't let anything happen to me. It sounds crazy, but I was…calm. Confident. Sure, there were a couple of bleak moments, but more than that, Jonah made me feel safe. I knew he could handle anything."

Naomi simply stared at her, a bemused smile playing on her lips.

"What?" Ellie demanded.

"You know what," her sister chided. "I've seen the way he looks at you. He's falling for you—hard. The only question in my mind was whether you felt the same—and whether it matters."

"What do you mean, whether it matters?"

Naomi arched a brow. "Unless you're considering a long-distance relationship, it's irrelevant. You'll be on a plane in a matter of weeks."

Ellie bit her bottom lip. She'd been waiting for the right moment to tell her sister. She supposed this one was as good as any.

"Actually, there's been a change of plans."

"Okay," her sister said slowly.

"I'm still going to Los Angeles…but only for two weeks."

Naomi frowned. "What?"

"I decided to take the teaching contract at Francis Murdoch."

Her sister blinked, then shook her head as if to clear it. "I'm confused. What's going on?"

"It's hard to put it all in words. I've been thinking a lot lately about Mom, about Orchard Hill, and about what I really want, what would *really* make me happy. And being honest? Jonah called me out. He said I wasn't truly running toward my dream, I was running away from my grief."

"Wow."

"He was absolutely right. Today, when I was packing up my desk, I was so relieved to be out of there—but not necessarily all that excited about where I was going. On paper I should be ecstatic, right? A role in a big-budget Hollywood movie—it's what I've wanted since I was a kid. But it all just felt…wrong. I left the building, and they'd lit this huge menorah in the plaza. The lights were like beacons in the darkness, bright and constant. This might sound silly, but I swear I heard Mom laugh."

Ellie watched her sister, waiting for her to roll her eyes or snort in disbelief.

Instead Naomi pursed her lips together, her eyes brimming.

"I hear her, too," Naomi whispered.

"Really?" The word came out squeaky and choked. Naomi nodded, and tears spilled down Ellie's cheeks.

"All she wanted was for us to be happy," Naomi urged.

"I know," Ellie replied, sniffing. "And I've been obsessed with crafting a fantasy of happiness. I was too scared to sit down and examine what's actually making me unhappy. The only way I could know what I wanted was to first acknowledge what was wrong, and that was terrifying, because the biggest problem in my life was not having Mom around. Nothing I can do will fix that."

"You're right—we can't bring her back. But we can do our best to be the family she taught us to be. Dan and the boys and I will always be here for you, no matter what you're doing or where you go. Do you believe me?"

"I do. And it's past time I set my fear aside and started returning the favor. That's why I called my agent and told him I couldn't relocate to LA."

"What did he say?"

Ellie laughed, still incredulous at how it had all worked out. "He said that's fine, they only need me for two weeks. They changed the script to have the two leads go on vacation together, and now most of the movie will be shot on location in the Caribbean."

"Seriously? That's fantastic! And the teaching job? You spoke to the principal?"

"She was fine with it, said getting a substitute for two weeks was a bargain compared to having a real-life, sort-of Hollywood actress in the drama program."

Naomi briefly clapped her hands over her mouth, and when she lowered them, she fixed Ellie with a huge grin. "Aunt Ellie is going to teach at Francis Murdoch. Gideon and Isaac will be beside themselves."

"Hopefully they won't be sick of me by then, considering I'll need to crash at their house while I look for somewhere to live in Orchard Hill." Ellie gave her sister an exaggeratedly wide, innocent smile, batting her lashes to boot.

Naomi slung her arm across Ellie's shoulders. "You can stay as long as you want. We'd love to have you."

Ellie pulled her sister into a hug. For the first time in years, her life felt ordered and right. She had a plan she was excited about, a future she could look forward to, and all was well in her world.

Well, almost all.

As if on cue Naomi said, "Jonah is going to be so happy you're staying. When are you going to tell him?"

Ellie winced. "I wouldn't bet on him being thrilled. Last night we had...words."

"Please. I've seen the way he looks at you, even before he literally dragged you from a burning car. He's fallen harder than a bowling ball rolling off a skyscraper."

"He was just doing his job," Ellie retorted, but her heart swelled and lifted ever so slightly, as if it were a balloon slowly filling with helium.

"He seems like a great guy. Whatever you said to each other, I'm sure you can work it out." Naomi smiled and patted Ellie's arm.

"Sorry to bother you."

Ellie and Naomi turned in unison to greet the nurse poking her head around the edge of the curtain.

"Miss Bloom, you have some visitors in the lobby. Normally we'd ask them to wait until you were discharged, but on this occasion your doctor said we can make a brief exception, if you'd like to pop out and say hello."

The sisters exchanged quizzical glances.

"Visitors?" Ellie echoed. "Plural?"

The nurse smiled secretively as she held back the curtain. "Right this way."

Ellie shrugged at her sister, who looked equally bewildered, and then followed the nurse back down the hall to the lobby. She pushed through the door—and immediately slapped her hands over her mouth in astonishment.

The entire, still-costumed cast of the Hanukkah play, along with scores of parents, Rabbi Spellman, and of course Jonah himself had assembled in the otherwise empty lobby. Upon seeing her, the kids parted to reveal that they'd brought the menorah from the finale—a cardboard and papier mâché creation topped with electric candles repurposed from an old chandelier in Noa's store.

Before she could utter more than a delighted squeak, the

kids launched into the final scene of the play—lighting the menorah as they took turns explaining why the tradition continues to be observed.

One by one they pretended to light each lamp—while secretly one of the older kids switched the candles on from behind—and pronounced their line to an audience that now included several nurses, two doctors, and both of the admitting receptionists.

It hadn't been easy blending her style and ambitions with Jonah's, especially not with the specter of her mother haunting every choice she made, not to mention the looming pressure of Rabbi Spellman's expectations. But as she watched the kids perform her eyes stung with fresh tears as undiluted pride threatened to overwhelm her.

Some of the kids spoke haltingly, others with ease and fluidity, but every single child exuded confidence, and that satisfied Ellie more than anything.

Over the heads of the performers and their parents Ellie found Jonah, standing at the back of the group, arms folded across his chest. Their eyes met.

He smiled.

All at once Ellie felt still. Calm and collected and quiet, sedate with peace she hadn't known since her mother's diagnosis years ago.

She'd made the right decision. Everything was about to change for the better. She just knew it.

Chapter Seventeen

B Y THE TIME her sister turned the corner toward the house the clock on the dashboard showed minutes 'til midnight. Although the impromptu performance received rave reviews from the hospital staff, unfortunately it didn't make Ellie's test results come back any faster. She'd waved fondly to the departing crowd before returning to her curtained purgatory, finally to be given a clean bill of health another couple of hours later.

As Naomi headed toward the driveway the headlights of her car swung along the front of the house, illuminating a figure perched on the front steps.

"Who on earth is sitting out there at this time of night?" Naomi asked, but Ellie recognized him the moment she saw him.

"Jonah," she answered promptly.

Naomi shot her an intrigued glance across the car, then pulled up to the garage and killed the engine.

"I'll see you inside," her sister told her, her tone practically screaming that she would expect a fully detailed recap of this late-night, front-step rendezvous.

Ellie nodded, then walked in the opposite direction to the front of the house, her heart pounding harder with every step. Was he just here to check that she was all right? Was he still angry? Maybe he wanted to clear the air and plan the way forward as friends—only friends. What if he wasn't happy about her decision to stay in Orchard Hill? What if he thought she was mercurial, emotional, unable to make clear choices? What if he dismissed anything she said to him as one of her ever-changing moods? What if she told him how she really felt and he simply walked away?

"Hi," she said timidly when she reached him, having talked herself into uncharacteristic paranoia and nerves. He looked weary and cold, shoulders hunched, coat zipped all the way up to his chin, and she braced herself for a punishing conclusion to yesterday's argument.

Instead Jonah smiled, though his expression was guarded. "How are you feeling?"

"Right as rain," she replied with forced brightness. "No broken bones, internal injuries, nada. Evidently I am concussed, so I have to take it easy for the next couple of days. Nothing physically or intellectually demanding, and no screen time, so I'm looking forward to several hours on the couch catching up on podcasts."

"That's good news," he said softly.

She studied him for a moment, trying to read him, but his face was inscrutable. She couldn't tell whether he was working himself up to say something, or waiting for her to speak, so she took advantage of the gap.

"Clearly I owe you a huge thank-you, and by huge I mean I don't know any words in any language that would be sufficient. You saved my life, Jonah."

He'd taken an interest in his clasped hands as she spoke, and acknowledged her words with a slight lift of his shoulder. "The delivery driver did, too. If he hadn't seen the car and run to the temple…"

He trailed off, evidently deciding that the likely outcome was better left unsaid.

"I'll thank him when I see him, but right now I'm here with you. And I'm incredibly grateful."

He still didn't look up, but he patted the space beside him on the step. She eased down next to him, her breath catching as she caught his scent.

Icicles and nighttime and the limitless firmament.

"I'm sorry about last night. I'd had a rough day and my temper was short." He met her gaze suddenly, his eyes as dark and clear as the sky overhead.

She shook her head firmly. "Don't be. It was my fault. I pressed you, you told me what you thought, and I couldn't handle it. I would say we should pretend the whole thing never happened, but the truth is, I needed to hear what you said."

He winced. "I was harsh."

"You were right. I was running away."

"You were right, too," he admitted. "For all my big talk

about choosing my own path and making my own choices, I tethered my happiness to whether or not my dad approved. I was a total hypocrite. I see that now, thanks to you."

"Not sure I can really accept any credit, but either way I'm glad you've realized that you're pretty damn awesome, no matter what your dad thinks."

He smiled reluctantly. "Thanks. And, as it happens, I think my dad might be starting to lean that way, too."

"Really?" She sat up straighter. "Did he say something? Did you guys talk?"

"He liked the play. And the dramatic rescue didn't hurt, either."

Ellie clapped her hands together in delight. "That's wonderful, Jonah. I know you'll be able to get back to where you were eventually."

"I hope so," Jonah replied, sounding more optimistic than she'd ever heard him.

He shifted his weight slightly, and she knew this was it— he was gearing up to talk about the issue hovering above their heads like a storm cloud.

Her move to Los Angeles.

She decided to head him off.

"I quit my job today," she informed him.

His shoulders slumped, but he attempted a smile, and the effort alone was enough to shove her over the cliff and fall headfirst in love.

Except she already loved him, she realized. She'd been

falling for him since the moment they met and now, on this cold brick step in the middle of the night, she was utterly, irretrievably, never-to-surface-again, deeply in love with this man.

"Congratulations," he said, resignation thick in his voice. "I appreciate you've wanted this for a long time, and I wish you all the best. Really, Ellie."

"I know you do. My sister and her family, too. In fact, I think most of Orchard Hill will be rooting for me when they find out. Which is why I've decided to stay."

He blinked. "What?"

She reached over and took his hand, linking her fingers through his, gambling that he wouldn't pull away.

He didn't.

"I accepted the teaching job, with permission to spend a couple of weeks in Los Angeles to film the movie. If my handful of lines vault me to superstardom, well, I'll cross that bridge when I come to it, but for now, I'm not going anywhere."

"Why?" Jonah asked, then quickly added, "I mean, obviously that's great. Amazing, actually. But what made you change your mind?"

"You," she told him firmly, her eyes never leaving his. "What you said and, more importantly, who you are. A future in Orchard Hill only became a possibility when I imagined you in it."

He squeezed her hand, reached to take her other one,

too. "I know we only met a week ago, but I've fallen for you, Ellie. Maybe I came to Orchard Hill for the wrong reasons, but with you here, I'll stay for the right ones."

She beamed up at him, at his serious expression, at the only man who'd ever made her feel this happy. Suddenly he broke into a broad grin.

"Now that we've got the talking out of the way, can I kiss you?"

She laughed, slinging her arms around his neck. "Yes, please."

His lips found hers and instantly the rest of the world fell away. There was only the delicious pressure of his mouth, the reassuring weight and warmth of his arms around her waist, the knowledge that he was hers, and they had so much joy ahead of them.

The future didn't look like she'd imagined, but that was okay. This version was better.

Jonah pulled back, then pressed his forehead against hers.

"It's the last night of Hanukkah, and I haven't lit the candles yet. Want to come upstairs?"

She kissed him again. And again. And once more before nodding. "Let's go."

Jonah took Ellie by the hand and led her the short distance to his own front steps. Together they climbed the brick stairs and went inside, the front door falling shut behind them.

Were an observer to pass along the deserted sidewalk,

walking softly so as not to disturb the hushed, darkened, sleeping houses, they might chance to look up at the most handsome—if somewhat tattered—house on the block. In the center window on the second floor, the onlooker might spy a brass menorah lit by nine brilliant, blazing candles, their light proudly piercing the darkness.

And if this silent passerby paused, perhaps buttoning their coat against the winter air, or simply to enjoy the comforting glow of Hanukkah, they might just see two people in love. Sharing an embrace, exchanging kisses, smiling into the promise of their limitless future.

Epilogue

JONAH WALKED THROUGH the front door and immediately shucked his jacket, then hung it on the hook and dropped his heavy duffel to the floor. He kicked off his shoes and took two steps toward the kitchen, then turned back, bent down, and moved his shoes into their place in the little cubby Ellie had set up.

"Ellie, I'm home," he called. Then he paused, sniffed, and walked faster. "Is something burning?"

"No," she called back, and then added, "Maybe."

He'd barely made it out of the entranceway when the smoke alarm went off, squealing directly above his head. He jogged the rest of the way into the kitchen and found Ellie pulling a sheet of what looked like blackened coasters out of the oven.

"This isn't going quite to plan," she shouted over the alarm, dropping the sheet onto the counter. Jonah reached past her to shove open the window, then grabbed a dish towel and began waving it in front of the sensor, clearing the air so it finally shut off.

Ellie was waiting for him when he got back to the kitchen.

"Hi," she said innocently, pushing up on her tiptoes to kiss him. "How was your day?"

"Suddenly seeming a lot less stressful by comparison. What culinary escapade are you on this evening?"

"St. Patrick's Day cookies for the teachers' lounge." Ellie scowled at the charred discs on the sheet.

"I have it on good authority that prepackaged ones from the grocery store are equally as delicious."

"But do they come in personalized leprechaun shapes unique to each member of staff?"

"Probably not," Jonah admitted, smiling at the utterly characteristic image of Ellie painstakingly cutting cookie dough to resemble her colleagues—and then burning them beyond recognition.

Life with Ellie certainly never lacked excitement. He'd missed her terribly while she was in Los Angeles, but he couldn't wait to see her on the big screen, and the news of her part had raised her profile in the local theater scene to the point that she could pretty much pick and choose how and when she wanted to be involved. The principal at Francis Murdoch was already hinting strongly that she'd be offered a permanent contract in the fall, and in the meantime she had a busy schedule of productions booked through the spring and summer.

Coming home to her was the bright spot of every day— even the darkest ones. Now that he'd left the fire department to work as a paramedic full-time his work lay heavier on his shoulders, but nothing lightened the load like Ellie's smile.

Even if it was accompanied by a smoke alarm.

"I guess I need to start over," Ellie said glumly, propping her hands on her hips. "I'll have to go next door again and ask my sister if she has any butter."

"Again?"

"I had to go over earlier to ask if she had any eggs. And then flour. And then I popped over for two teensy, tiny minutes to borrow some vanilla extract."

He grinned, sliding the destroyed cookies into the trash. "Next time you should just cook in her kitchen. Maybe her smoke detector is less sensitive."

"But who would greet you when you came home?" Ellie moved behind him and rubbed his back, pressing her thumbs between his shoulder blades.

Jonah groaned with pleasure. "You're absolutely right. Flour, milk, stand mixer—you should definitely haul it all over here."

She worked a few more knots out of his muscles, then swung around to face him, her arm on his waist. "Can you handle dinner? I really do need to come up with something for the teachers' lounge, even if it's only a trip to the bakery."

"Of course." He dropped a kiss on her lips, then opened the fridge and sized up the possibilities.

She took out a clean glass bowl, cracked two eggs into it, and then poured in an unmeasured amount of flour. He tried not to watch.

"Do your parents like shortbread?" she asked over her shoulder.

Oh, Ellie, there's no way that concoction will result in shortbread.

"Sure," he said, pulling a variety of vegetables out of the fridge and then getting to work chopping them up.

"I'll make a couple extra for them. We can bring them on Saturday when we go for dinner."

Jonah smiled to himself, imagining his parents delicately biting into Ellie's version of cookies, then forcing exaggerated grins before discreetly tossing them in the trash. Although his relationship with his dad was on the mend, he had to hand it to her—she made every encounter with them ten times more relaxed and fun.

"They'll love it," he promised.

She beamed, and he couldn't help himself. He dropped the handful of carrots he'd been arranging on the chopping board, crossed the kitchen, and swept her into his arms.

Ellie giggled as she landed against his chest, and slid her hands up to his shoulders. "Don't try to distract me. These cookies are getting made if it takes me all night."

"I would never. Just needed a little sweetness of my own." He kissed her, long and lingering, tangling his hand in her strawberry-blond hair.

After a minute Ellie smiled up at him, her eyes bright and sparkling. "I love you something terrible, you know that?"

"Of course. I love you, too. But feel free to remind me anytime."

"I will," she promised, tilting her face up for another kiss.

He brought his lips to hers once more, marveling that the happiness he'd spent so long working to find had found him, instead. Neither of them had to run ever again—they were exactly where they belonged.

Together.

The End

Want more? Check out another Rebecca Crowley romance, *Insider*!

Join Tule Publishing's newsletter for more great reads and weekly deals!

If you enjoyed *Shine a Light*, you'll love the next book in…

The Orchard Hill series

Book 1: *Shine a Light*

Book 2: *Coming in April 2022!*

Available now at your favorite online retailer!

More books by Rebecca Crowley

The London Phoenix series

Book 1: *Insider*

Book 2: *Undercover*

Book 3: *Off the Record*

Available now at your favorite online retailer!

About the Author

Rebecca Crowley inherited her love of romance from her mom, who taught her to at least partially judge a book by the steaminess of its cover. She writes contemporary romance with smart heroines and swoon-worthy heroes, and never tires of the happily-ever-after. Having pulled up her Kansas roots to live in New York City, London and Johannesburg, Rebecca currently resides in Houston.

Thank you for reading

Shine a Light

If you enjoyed this book, you can find more from all our great authors at TulePublishing.com, or from your favorite online retailer.

TULE
PUBLISHING